Gabe tore a paper towel from the roll and dabbed gently at her eyes. His fingers still circled her wrist, warming her.

He set aside the wad of paper, but he didn't let her go. He leaned closer across the counter, his thumb stroking her cheek. She felt the moisture trail as he swiped away a tear that had spilled down her face.

He'll let go now, she thought, although she didn't want to lose the contact. But as his hand lingered against her cheek, she couldn't resist the impulse to press in to it, to feel his palm cup her face.

"Lori."

She couldn't resist the demand of her softly spoken name. She opened her eyes, then stared, stunned by the sharpness of his desire. An answering flame flared inside her....

Dear Reader,

We're deep into spring, and the season and romance always seem synonymous to me. So why not let your reading reflect that? Start with Sherryl Woods's next book in THE ROSE COTTAGE SISTERS miniseries, *The Laws of Attraction*. This time it's Ashley's turn to find love at the cottage—which the hotshot attorney promptly does, with a man who appears totally different from the cutthroat lawyers she usually associates with. But you know what they say about appearances....

Karen Rose Smith's *Cabin Fever* is the next book in our MONTANA MAVERICKS: GOLD RUSH GROOMS continuity, in which a handsome playboy and his beautiful secretary are hired to investigate the mine ownership issue. But they're snowbound in a cabin...and work can only kill so much time! And in *Lori's Little Secret* by Christine Rimmer, the next of her BRAVO FAMILY TIES stories, a young woman who was always the shy twin has a big secret (two, actually): seven years ago she pretended to be her more outgoing sister—which resulted in a night of passion and a baby, now child. And said child's father is back in town... Judy Duarte offers another of her BAYSIDE BACHELORS, in *Worth Fighting For*, in which a single adoptive mother—with the help of her handsome neighbor, who's dealing with a loss of his own—grapples with the possibility of losing her child. In Elizabeth Harbison's hilarious new novel, a young woman who wonders how to get her man finds help in a book entitled, well, *How To Get Your Man*. But she's a bit confused about which man she really wants to get! And in *His Baby to Love* by Karen Sandler, a long-recovered alcoholic needs to deal with her unexpected pregnancy, so she gratefully accepts her friend's offer of her chalet for the weekend. But she gets an unexpected roommate—the one man who'd pointed her toward recovery...and now has some recovering of his own to do.

So enjoy, and we'll see you next month, when things once again start to heat up, in Silhouette Special Edition!

Sincerely yours,

Gail Chasan
Senior Editor

Please address questions and book requests to:
Silhouette Reader Service
U.S.: 3010 Walden Ave., P.O. Box 1325, Buffalo, NY 14269
Canadian: P.O. Box 609, Fort Erie, Ont. L2A 5X3

HIS BABY TO LOVE
KAREN SANDLER

Silhouette

SPECIAL EDITION

Published by Silhouette Books

America's Publisher of Contemporary Romance

To those who struggle in the dark,
searching for a way back to the light.

 SILHOUETTE BOOKS

ISBN 0-373-24686-2

HIS BABY TO LOVE

Copyright © 2005 by Karen Sandler

This edition published by arrangement with Harlequin Books S.A.

® and TM are trademarks of Harlequin Books S.A., used under license.
Trademarks indicated with ® are registered in the United States Patent
and Trademark Office, the Canadian Trade Marks Office and in other
countries.

Visit Silhouette Books at www.eHarlequin.com

Printed in U.S.A.

Books by Karen Sandler

Silhouette Special Edition

The Boss's Baby Bargain #1488
Counting on a Cowboy #1572
A Father's Sacrifice #1636
His Baby To Love #1686

KAREN SANDLER

first caught the writing bug at age nine when, as a horse-crazy fourth grader, she wrote a poem about a pony named Tony. Many years of hard work later, she sold her first book (and she got that pony—although his name is Ben). She enjoys writing novels, short stories and screenplays and has produced two short films. She lives in Northern California with her husband of twenty-three years and two sons who are busy eating her out of house and home. You can reach Karen at karen@karensandler.net.

The Serenity Prayer

God, grant me the serenity
to accept the things I cannot change;
the courage to change the things I can;
and the wisdom to know the difference.

Prologue

Lori Jarret staggered through the swinging doors of the Two-Step Saloon and tried to focus on the row of cars in the small parking lot. She'd left her Mercedes SUV parked between a pickup and a small sedan, she was sure of it. But somehow all the cars kept swapping places in her line-of-sight, blurring and wobbling as she sought out the bulky vehicle she'd driven here.

Three drinks. She'd only had three—two Long Islands and a Gold Cadillac. The wine she'd drunk before the cowboy at the bar bought her those three— they just didn't count. Neither did the tequila chasers. She was plenty sober enough to drive.

Next thing she knew, she was slumped against the SUV, trying to stab her key into the lock. She couldn't remember finding her car or crossing the parking lot to get to it. Never mind, she was here. She just had to turn the key—

At the *whoop* of her car alarm, she stumbled back, staring stupidly at the car. She didn't recall setting the alarm, but then she wasn't really sure when she'd arrived, or how long she'd been here. Fumbling with the alarm button on her key chain, she deactivated it, slumping with relief against the car.

She didn't even hear the man coming toward her, didn't know he was there until he put a hand on her shoulder. She should have been scared, but she felt numb—pain, grief, despair airbrushed out of her by the alcohol. That was the whole point of drinking, anyway. Let the booze solve the problems she couldn't.

"Lady." The guy shook her a little. "You're too damn drunk to drive."

"Can drive jus' fine."

She tried to get a good look at his face, but it kept swimming past her, looping in a crazy circle. She caught the gleam of a badge on his chest, the police cap on his head. Her scrambled brain made out the word Marbleville on the cap before the letters all swam together.

"No way I'm letting you behind the wheel, lady." He snatched her keys from the Mercedes and activated the alarm again. "I'll give you a ride home."

"Not home." She shook her head and her world spun. "Stayin' at a hotel."

A strong hand on her arm, he led her to his patrol car. "In Marbleville? Or Hart Valley?"

Grief crept up inside her, despite the alcohol. "Not Har' Valley. Daughter hates me. Doesn' wan' me."

"Marbleville, then. Which place are you at?"

"Key in my purse."

Even with his hand guiding her, she tripped on a rough patch and her knees gave way. His grip tightened, and he pulled her back to her feet.

"Thanks," Lori muttered, the end of the word stretching out like a hiss.

"For what?" He had a nice voice, low and rumbling.

"Kep' me from falling."

They finally reached the cruiser and he leaned her against it while he opened the back door. Tugging her purse strap over her head, he settled her in the back and secured a seat belt across her. "Don't toss your cookies on my seats."

The door slammed shut, then the engine roared to life. That surprised her; she thought he was still standing beside the car.

Then he pulled out of the parking lot, and the world spiraled out of control again. "Sick," she gasped.

"Damn, damn, damn." The cruiser lurched to a stop and she struggled to keep from heaving in her lap. He reached her side in an instant, easing her legs out of the car, bending her head between her knees. She disgraced herself there in the gutter, barely missing the legs of her designer jeans. His hand remained on her shoulder, rubbing gently as she shuddered.

Handing her a towel to wipe her face, he produced a bottle of water. "Drink it all."

As he seat-belted her in again she trembled, clutching the water bottle as if it were a lifeline. She dozed as he drove, was vaguely aware of his support as they walked to her room. When she finally collapsed on her bed, she caught the briefest glimpse of him standing over her, a trace of sympathy in his implacable face. Then she fell unconscious again, her savior forgotten in her alcoholic haze.

Chapter One

Two Years Later

Hands clenching the wheel of her Honda Civic, Lori Jarret followed the twists of the asphalt-paved easement road, searching for the driveway to her friend Sadie's lakeside chalet. The thick forest of pines, cedars and redwoods lined the road on either side, filtering the last of the day's sunshine. Yellow beams speared through the canopy of trees, dotting the dark pavement with light.

The trip from the Bay Area to South Lake Tahoe had been a piece of cake. She'd gotten out of the city by two and the traffic was sparse on Interstate 80 and Highway 50. The late-spring weather was perfect, the skies clear and brilliant blue after an early morning rain.

But the closer she drew to Sadie's chalet, the tighter the tension wound inside Lori. As she traversed the last few dozen yards it was all she could do to continue forward instead of turning tail and running.

Most people escaped to the mountains to relax. Lori had come here to confront her demons.

She finally spotted the driveway, one of three feeding from the easement road, and made the turn. The

graveled drive led to a large parking area in front of
the sprawling one-story cedar and glass house. A
flight of stairs led up to a broad redwood deck that
wrapped around the chalet. Incense cedars and ponderosa pines surrounded the house on three sides, the
fourth side overlooking the crystalline blue waters of
Lake Tahoe.

Lori had been here once before, had made a fool
of herself at a party on the back deck. She'd nearly
upended herself over the waist-high railing, would
have plummeted down the hillside that dropped
sharply behind the chalet if Sadie's husband Tyrell
hadn't grabbed her just in time.

The memory only added to Lori's anxiety, setting
off a churning in her stomach. Maybe this wasn't
such a great idea after all. She'd thought two weeks
away from the city, beyond the pull of the old and familiar, would have cleared her mind and lightened her
heart. Instead, it just seemed to remind her of the
nightmare her life had once been.

She pulled up next to the pickup that no doubt belonged to the handyman Sadie said Tyrell had hired
to do some work around the chalet. Sadie had intended to talk to her husband about postponing the repairs to the deck and plumbing until after Lori's visit.
Apparently the handyman hadn't gotten the word
yet—no doubt due to Sadie's crazy hours as a surgi-
cal nurse and Tyrell's even crazier hours as an LAPD
detective.

The strap to her Hermès bag slung over her shoulder, Lori eased from the silver sedan and started for
the stairs. Her sensible rubber-soled sneakers thudded
softly on the redwood steps as she climbed them. Her

lungs, accustomed to a sea-level atmosphere and still recovering from a decade of cigarettes, labored in the thinner mountain air.

Exhaustion lay heavily on her shoulders as she fumbled in her bag for Sadie's key ring. She still had the suitcase to retrieve from the trunk, but simply couldn't face another trip down and then up the stairs. She could think only of finding a bed and dropping down onto it for a desperately needed nap. It seemed she spent half the daytime hours napping, trying to make up for the restless nights of broken sleep *and* the new demands on her body.

Pushing the front door open, Lori stepped into the spacious great room with its high vaulted ceilings and warm wood paneling. To her right, two plush sofas sat angled toward an entertainment unit complete with television, DVD and stereo system. A woodstove with a stack of split oak beside it sat near enough to warm the conversation area.

A dining table had been set up on the other side of the room, with the kitchen just beyond it. A wet bar stood in the corner between kitchen and dining area, bottles visible inside the glass-fronted cabinet. She blanked her mind before she could even think about what those bottles were filled with and turned her focus away.

Her stomach rumbled and she realized she hadn't eaten since breakfast when she'd only nibbled on rye toast. She'd intended to stop at the Safeway in South Lake Tahoe to pick up a few groceries, but when she'd pulled into town she didn't have the energy for even that simple chore. Doubtless there were a few staples in the kitchen—some soup, maybe some crackers. But even heating a can of soup seemed beyond her.

She slid the chain lock into place on the front door, then pointed herself toward the master bedroom. Door shut behind her, she scanned the comfortable room. A thick comforter in forest-green swirled with cream covered the king-size bed. Sliding French doors led out to the deck and the last few rays of the sun gilded the gold trim on the fireplace opposite the bed. The blond oak dresser and nightstands matched the four-poster. A smaller entertainment unit beside the dresser housed a television and DVD player.

Swinging her purse to the dresser, she turned the thumb lock on the bedroom door. No doubt the handyman had keys to the house; Lori would just as soon the man not intrude on her privacy while she was napping.

The soft mattress and plump pillows felt heavenly when she eased herself under the comforter. If she could keep the usual invasion of remorse and second thoughts at bay, she would be able to sleep.

But in the quiet of the room, the faint soughing of the wind outside a bare whisper, a familiar companion closed in—regret. The mistakes she'd made, memories of the people she'd hurt badly hounded her. And the centerpiece of her shame: the irremediable wounds she'd inflicted on her own daughter.

She wouldn't cry. She'd manipulated her world with tears and tantrums for far too long and it had led her to one disaster after another. Everyone who had given in to her, from her parents and sister to her ex-husband, had done her no favors. There was no one here to catch her—and it was time she stopped expecting someone to break her fall.

Breathing deeply, she did her best to wash away the

guilt, turning her focus briefly to the eighth of the twelve steps. *Become willing to make amends*... If there was any way to make amends, if she hadn't burned those bridges completely.

As she finally drifted off, a distant memory lingered, a thin thread maintaining consciousness. A man holding tight to her arm, guiding her, keeping her from stumbling into darkness. She hadn't thought of him since that night, had had too many days soaked in gin and whiskey intervening before she finally crawled toward the light. But somehow, his nearly forgotten face swam in her mind's eye a moment before she let herself slide into sleep.

With Lake Tahoe reflecting the sun setting behind him, Gabe Walker stopped along the mountain trail to reposition the fishing pole on his shoulder and shift the stringer of fish to his other hand. Just as well he'd left the tackle box behind at the chalet, and instead stuffed its contents into the multitude of pockets of his fishing vest.

He hadn't expected to catch his limit of trout within the first hour dunking his line in that private little cove below Sadie and Tyrell King's chalet. As it was, once he'd maxed out at five, he'd dunked the stringer of rainbows and Mackinaws back into the water and just sat back against a boulder to drink in the quiet.

Only his second day at the Tahoe house and he'd already released some of the ever-present tension he'd brought with him. It wasn't in him to ever completely relax, but the soothing brilliant blue of the lake, the midweek quiet rarely broken by a passing motorboat, had eased the worst of the knots inside him. He had a lonely night to get through, but maybe he'd see if the Kings' satellite dish could pick up the Giants game.

An unexpected stab of pain stopped him in his tracks. He'd always intended to take Brandon to a Dodgers game, had just about counted the days until his son would be old enough to appreciate the finer points of baseball. They'd watched the games on TV, Brandon cheering when Gabe cheered, even when the toddler hadn't a clue what was happening on the screen. Gabe kept telling himself, one more year and Brandon would be old enough. One more year.

Gabe pushed aside the memories and continued the serpentine climb up the hill toward the chalet. His rapid pace had him gasping for breath. He was fit enough, but the thinner air still didn't do his lungs any favors. Hart Valley in Marbleville County, where he patrolled as deputy sheriff, was only about fifteen hundred feet elevation. He was nearly a mile higher here. It didn't help that the shoulder holster for his semiautomatic constricted his chest with each breath.

By the time he reached the clearing where the chalet stood, his heart thundered in his ears. Grateful to be on level ground again, he crunched across the thick pine needles carpeting the sparse back lawn. The deck steps groaned and squeaked under his hiking boots, the sound reminding him of one of the myriad of chores he'd promised Tyrell he'd get to during his two-week stint here. He'd given himself permission to be lazy the first few days, only taking a cursory look around to see what needed doing. Starting tomorrow, he'd have to dig in.

Leaning the fishing pole against the wall beside the back door, Gabe dug in his jeans pocket for the set of keys Tyrell had given him. Despite the six years he'd spent in sleepy little Hart Valley in the Sierra Nevada foothills, he still had the instincts of an L.A. cop. He'd never quite been able to bring himself to leave the doors unlocked when he left his house. Even here where the nearest neighbor was invisible behind a cloak of trees and the chalet itself was so far off the beaten path you'd have to be lost to find it, he'd made sure the front and back doors were secure.

Shucking his fishing vest, he left it and the fishing pole outside. He flipped on the light by the door, then carried the stringer into the kitchen and dropped the gleaming trout into the sink. As he tried to remember where the knives were, his gaze strayed briefly to the great room beyond. He froze as his senses registered something amiss.

The chain lock was in place on the front door. The door to the bedroom he'd used last night was shut. He knew damn well he hadn't shut that door or used the chain—he knew better than to trust its false security.

Someone else was in the house. Rifling through the contents of the bedroom, no doubt, hoping the chain-lock and the closed bedroom door would slow Gabe down. An escape onto the deck through the bedroom slider would be easy, the door plenty big to allow a thief to carry out the television and DVD. Likely, Tyrell's wife Sadie didn't keep jewelry here, so the thief's take would be limited to the electronics in the one room.

Maybe they intended to come back out here for the large-screen television and stereo in the great room once they got the bedroom cleaned out. They wouldn't follow through on that plan now that he was here.

Moving quietly across the great room in the dimming light, Gabe pulled his 9 mm free as he reached for the bedroom door. Ear pressed against the hollow core wood surface, he listened. Silence. Maybe the thieves had been here and gone. They could have had a lookout watching for his return.

He tried the bedroom door. The damn thing was locked. He gave the knob another twist just to be sure. It didn't budge. The hollow core door with its substandard thumb-lock would be easy enough to break down, but there was an easier solution—a small key kept on the lip of the molding above the door. He'd discovered the special purpose key when he'd first arrived. With his police background, he'd never quite shaken the mindset that every room could be a potential crime scene and he habitually swept any new space with a quick once-over.

Reaching for the slender key, he fitted it into the lock and quietly released it. The knob gave way and he eased the door open slowly. Still no sound from inside. He opened the door wider, the Glock ready in his hand, but the room appeared empty.

Until he opened the door far enough to see the bed. Curled up under the covers, her silky hair spread across the pillows, was the most gorgeous blonde he'd ever seen.

One moment Lori Jarret was so deep in dreams she would have thought she was lost to the world. The next she was wide-awake, heart stuttering in her chest.

A prickling sensation crept down her arms and she knew someone was in the room with her. The fears and confusion that had driven her to the Tahoe chalet faded to insignificance as she experienced true terror. She had to force herself to turn, to see who stood beside the bed. Then he turned on the light on the nightstand and she had to squeeze her eyes shut a moment to adjust to the glare.

When she opened her eyes again, she thought her heart would jump from her chest. *Oh my God! He's got a gun!* The weapon filled her field of view; she couldn't see anything else. Even the hand holding it was out of focus. The enormous barrel gaped at her.

She could barely get enough breath to speak. "Please don't hurt me." She risked a quick glance up at his face and could swear guilt flickered briefly in his hard green eyes.

He kept the gun steady on her. "Let's see your hands."

Shaking, she pulled her hands free of the comforter and held them aloft. "Whatever you want, take it and go."

She felt nearly sick with horror when he reached for her, groping her under the covers from the waist down. Then she realized there was nothing sexual about his impersonal touch.

He was patting her down for a weapon. She'd suffered that indignity only once when she'd been stopped in San Francisco. The officer had been just as impersonal and more than apologetic when he'd realized whose daughter she was.

Apparently, the man was satisfied she wasn't packing heat and his gun vanished. Now that the object of her terror was gone, she could shift her gaze higher to the man who had held it. She took in broad shoulders in a long-sleeve heather-gray Henley, a pale brown leather holster crisscrossing his well-muscled chest and a day's worth of beard on a roughly handsome face. There was something familiar about those stark cheekbones, those sharp green eyes, but recognition eluded her.

He leaned in closer. "Now suppose you tell me what the hell you're doing here."

She wasn't about to respond to his demand until he answered her questions. "What are *you* doing here? And why do you have a gun?"

"I'm a cop." Impatiently he reached in his back pocket. The Marbleville County deputy sheriff's badge he flashed tickled another memory that Lori couldn't quite grasp.

She sat up, scrunching against her pillow. "Then you're not the handyman." She brought her knees up, instinctively wanting to protect her abdomen. "Have you seen him? Tyrell was supposed to tell him—"

"How do you know Tyrell?"

"I'm a friend of Sadie's." Her hands trembled and she locked them together across her shins. A familiar craving bubbled up inside her, but she pushed it aside. "Look, I appreciate you coming to check on things here, but you can leave now."

His jaw worked and his face grew harsher. "Is that right?"

She knew him, she was certain of it. On the heels of that realization came the anxiety that had haunted her every time she woke from a blackout—that she might have been intimate with a man during her drunken fugue and would have to face that man later. Could this be her nightmare come true? But if it was, wouldn't he recognize her?

It didn't bear thinking about. "Look," she told him, keeping her tone level despite her incipient fear, "Sadie invited me up here for a couple of weeks. She said Tyrell had arranged for a handyman to do repairs, but that he'd call the man and reschedule. So if you saw a man working around the house, that was him and he's gone now."

His gaze narrowed on her. "Do I know you?"

As humiliation washed over her, she had to resist the impulse to bury her face in her hands. "I don't think so," she said, the words faltering.

Two fingers under her chin, he tipped her head up, studied her face. His touch was gentle enough, but as impersonal as when he'd searched her. Still, the human contact felt good, too good.

She shrugged away from him. "I have one of those faces. I'm sorry, but I'd really like you to go now."

"Then we have a problem here." He shoved his hands into his pockets. "Tyrell promised me the chalet for two weeks. So if anyone's leaving, it's you."

The blonde kept looking his way as she spoke on his cell phone, her brown eyes accusatory. As if he'd done a damn thing wrong pulling his gun on her. How the hell was he supposed to know she was a friend of Sadie's? And although what he saw on the surface— a woman who seemed so delicate he could have snapped her in two—indicated she wouldn't be armed, he'd been fooled enough times as a rookie cop in L.A. that he'd learned to never make assumptions.

Better to search and find nothing than be deceived and dead.

He hadn't liked the terror in her eyes when she first woke to see him standing over her or her shudder of fear when he ran a hand over her body. Even though he must have surprised her, he was one of the good guys. People turned to him for help. Her expectation that he was going to hurt her put a bitter taste in his mouth.

She glanced his way again as she paced across the great room from the breakfast bar to the sofa. In the pale yellow light from the table lamps he'd switched on, her skin was an impossibly creamy shade, begging him to touch.

Thank God they'd left the bedroom, had come out here to neutral territory, so to speak. Warm and sleepy in her bed, golden hair tousled, she looked like a dream. Even fully dressed, the blonde was a threat to his equilibrium. He wasn't a saint by any means and it had been a long time since he'd been intimate with a woman.

And to have a woman as hot as this one appear out of the blue—it was like manna from heaven. If he had any interest in a quick, anonymous fling, that is, a little bedroom athletics. He could imagine that silky blond hair trailing across his skin, those rich brown eyes sparking into flame with the slightest touch. His fingers itched to start that fire.

But he liked to think he had more sense than that. While Lori Jarret didn't exactly look needy, there was something in that cool distant expression that sent up warning flags. Watch out—strings attached. Beware—this one has baggage.

He knew those warning flags well enough because

they'd clamored long and loud when he'd first met his ex-wife, Krista. Except he'd been too busy listening to his body's cravings to pay attention. Look at the hell that had led him into.

His gaze strafed the willowy blonde again, from her pale silky hair to the designer shoes on her feet. Lori Jarret—even her name sparked a vague memory when she'd introduced herself. He'd met her before, he was sure of it. Likely it was a traffic stop, long enough ago that even a woman as beautiful as her had left only a faint impression.

Even so, when he met her gaze as she flicked another glance his way, there was something deeper there that urged him to explore. He slammed the door on that temptation.

She hung up his cell and held it out to him. "Thanks. I didn't realize my battery was so low."

He took the phone and clipped it back on his belt. "So?"

Wrists crossed in front of her, her hands rested against her abdomen as she leaned against the breakfast bar. "There was a mix-up."

"I'd say so."

She tucked a strand of hair behind her ear. "When Tyrell told Sadie he'd arranged the repair of the deck and plumbing, she thought he'd hired a handyman, not asked a friend to help."

"Tyrell and I set this up a week ago—plenty of time to clear things up with Sadie."

"She's been slammed at the hospital and Tyrell's been pulling double shifts. They've barely seen each other. It wasn't until this morning they spoke face-to-face."

He'd shut off his own phone this morning, just wanting for the moment to be cut off from his life. That in itself had been a huge step for him. He never liked being too far from his phone, didn't want to risk missing that one crucial call that might put his life back together. It had been ten years, but sometimes miracles happened. Or so he'd been told.

"So, now what?"

She sighed, a world of discouragement in the sound. But when she met his gaze, nothing in her face betrayed weakness. "I'll head back home. You were here first, had the first invitation."

He could see the weight on those slender shoulders, had felt the same unbearable heaviness nearly every day of the past ten years. He desperately needed this brief sanctuary and shouldn't feel the slightest trace of guilt sending this woman back down the mountain.

And yet he did.

A noble impulse surfaced inside him—to defer to her, to head home and let her have the chalet. It wouldn't be a complete waste—he could take a couple days catching up with his own chores at his modest cabin. He'd had a standing invitation with Tyrell for years; he could always arrange another time to return to the chalet.

He knew full well he wouldn't, though. It had been hard enough persuading himself to take these two weeks.

She kept staring at him as if she was waiting for him to be the gentleman. As if she was used to crooking her little finger and having the world fall at her feet.

Damned if he would.

"Look, lady, I'm not the kind of guy who does favors for beautiful women."

Her mouth tightened. "Just as well. I don't need any favors."

Temptation bubbled up to stroke his thumb across those lips just to see them soften again. "Needy women tend to send me running in the other direction."

Color rose in her cheeks. "I'm not—" She turned away from him and headed toward the bedroom. "Just let me get my purse."

Something goaded him into going after her, stopping her. He put his hand on her shoulder and she felt even more frail than she looked. "You don't have to be in such a damn hurry."

Her gaze fell to his hand, then she shot him a look that told him there was an underpinning of steel beneath that fragile frame. "Let go of me."

He dropped his hand. "Sorry. I only meant…" What the hell had he meant? With her heat still lingering on his skin, he couldn't seem to clear his head. A sudden impulse to keep her here closed in on him, had him speaking before he could think.

"It's dark already. The roads aren't the greatest."

Her brown gaze narrowed. "I'm a careful driver."

Good, she gave him an out. He'd just leave it at that.

But the gremlin impulse kept pushing him. "Why not stay the night, leave in the morning?"

She stared at him, as if digging into his soul. "I don't think so."

Okay, fine. What did he care if she ran her car off one of the twists and turns of Highway 50? He stepped back and she moved away.

"The chalet has two other bedrooms." The words leaped out before he could stop them.

She turned. "I don't think—"

"I'll move my gear into the one at the far end of the hall, use the other bathroom." He took a step back, wanting to give her the space, wanting it himself.

Still she hesitated and he grew impatient. "Look, Lori, I don't care what you do. But if you're going to head home, you'd better get on the road now, before it gets any darker."

She tipped her head up. "If I stay…" He could see the movement of her throat as she swallowed. "You can't touch me again."

"I never meant to—" Except he couldn't quite forget the feel of her under his fingers. "I won't."

Finally she nodded. "I'll stay the night. Leave in the morning."

He stepped around her toward the bedroom. "I'll clear out my stuff."

As he edged past her, he caught another glimpse of her soft brown gaze and in an instant, the memory came clear. He remembered thinking at the time her pain must have been bone-deep for him to see it so plainly in her alcohol-fogged eyes.

He looked back at her over his shoulder, trying to connect the waifish blonde of today with the blowsy drunk of two years ago. He couldn't quite overlay the images, maybe because a part of him didn't want to. That woman from the parking lot of the Two-Step Saloon had never quite left his consciousness. Seeing her cold sober and in the flesh, he'd likely *never* forget her now.

Chapter Two

*H*e *remembered her.*

Lori saw it in Gabe Walker's face when he turned to look at her over his shoulder and his recognition triggered her own. That night at the cowboy bar in Marbleville, her almost too drunk to walk, let alone drive her SUV, him steady and sober keeping her from killing herself or someone else on the road.

A shadow still lingered of the agonizing pain she'd felt that night, the relentless hurt alcohol never could quite dull. She could still see the disappointment in her daughter Jessie's face, remembered the weary wisdom in those young eyes at being let down once again by her mother.

Lori had taken Gabe's rescue that night as her due—hadn't men always stepped in to save her from herself? But since then she'd learned a little bit about personal responsibility.

He slipped out of sight into the bedroom, leaving her stomach roiling as it always did when she encountered people from her old life. She'd left that environment behind her, and the people in it, knowing she wasn't strong enough yet to keep to her program when faced with reminders of how she'd been. Besides, most of them were still drinking, still hitting the bars.

Gabe reappeared with a canvas duffel bag slung over his shoulder. "All yours." He took a step toward the hallway.

"Gabe."

He turned, looked at her expectantly. Not a clue in his face as to what he was thinking. The knot in her stomach gripped tighter.

"I remember too," she said softly. "When you helped me…when I—" She looked away a moment, then back. "I'm not doing that anymore."

For a moment he just stared, then he nodded. "Okay." Just that one word, his tone neutral. Yet she heard his skepticism all the same.

She couldn't blame him. Who ever believed an alcoholic who says she'll never drink again? "I just wanted to acknowledge…" Her throat felt dry and she ached for just a sip. "To thank you—"

"I didn't do it for you." His steady gaze stripped her bare. "I did it for who you might hurt."

He might as well have stabbed her in the gut. It wasn't anything more than she deserved. She mustered a ghost of a smile. "Thank you anyway. For that."

Another brusque nod then he headed down the hallway. She felt utterly exhausted by the stew of emotions inside her coupled with her body's wrenching changes. Her mind dulled by the turmoil, she had to push herself out the front door to get her own things from the car.

The light on the front deck reached as far as the stairs, faded to near blackness by her car. She felt her way to the Civic's front door, opening it to pop the trunk. The dome light gave her enough illumination to safely make her way to the rear of the car.

Hidden by the open trunk lid, she sagged onto the Civic's bumper, overwhelmed. Maybe she ought to just go home now, curl up in her bed. Self-examination had never been her strong suit, had more often urged her to take a drink than to improve herself. Gabe's presence, even for just one night, only made matters worse. Facing someone who knew what she'd been, what she could still be if she strayed even the slightest bit from her program, added an excruciating edge to an impossible task.

She stared out into the darkness to where the driveway disappeared into the shadows of barely visible trees. She'd never liked driving at night, particularly on an unfamiliar road. Weighing the option of making her escape on a dark mountain road against confronting whatever demons Gabe's presence summoned, staying the night was clearly the correct choice. With any luck, he'd keep his distance and she would barely notice he was there.

But there was no luck left in her life. Just as she rose and leaned into the trunk for her suitcase, he appeared beside her. Startled, she jumped back and hit her wrist on the edge of the trunk.

"Sorry," he said, those green eyes as neutral as ever.

"No problem." She rubbed her wrist, trying to soothe the sting away. His gaze was still steady on her, appraising. He was only a couple inches taller than her five-ten—not a muscle-bound bodybuilder, but powerful nonetheless. He'd removed his shoulder holster, soothing that terror she'd felt facing his gun. That made the temptation to lean on him and let him make things easier for her that much stronger.

Why did he have to be so good-looking? He wasn't a pretty boy like the drop-dead gorgeous rat that had gotten her into her current fix. Even so, with those green eyes and good cheekbones, wide shoulders and ropy arms, his appeal tugged at her, made it hard to think about all the reasons that had brought her here.

Still rubbing her wrist, she edged around the back of the Civic. "Was there something you wanted?"

"You need help carrying in?"

Of course she did. Women always needed men to take care of them. She shook her head. "I only have the one suitcase." And the stack of books inside the car, books she'd just as soon he not see. She had nothing to be ashamed of, but that was one conversation she would just as soon not have with a stranger she wouldn't see again after tonight.

But before she could protest, he'd grabbed her battered Louis Vuitton. She ought to tell him no, but he was already halfway up the stairs. As tired as she was, she was grateful not to lug the heavy suitcase up the stairs. But she shouldn't have let him do it, should have made it clearer she didn't need his help.

He wasn't in the great room when she stepped inside, nor could she see him in the kitchen. Her Louis Vuitton had been set on the bed in the master bedroom.

Shutting the door behind her, she retrieved her toiletries bag from her suitcase and headed for the bathroom. She wasn't here to impress anyone but her hair looked a fright and her face was pale to the point of ghostly. A quick brush and some lipstick and she'd at least be halfway human.

When she returned to the great room, he was busy in the kitchen. He'd started a fire in the woodstove and with the early afternoon chill, the flickering flames were irresistible. She stood before the stove, working some warmth back into her icy hands.

"Do you need help?" she called out.

"You like cleaning trout?" He lifted a silvery fish from the sink and dropped it on a nearby cutting board.

Her stomach lurched and she counted the weeks. It seemed early for the nausea. "Not really."

He pressed the tip of his knife to the fish's belly. "Then I don't need help."

Lori looked away before he started slicing into the fish. "Excuse me. I forgot something." Hurrying for the bedroom, she shut the door and leaned against it. Gulping in air, she prayed her stomach's rebellion would subside.

Just as she'd decided she wouldn't have to run for the bathroom, Gabe knocked on the bedroom door. Lori eased it open. He stood there, his face impassive as always. "I caught more trout than I can eat. I hate to see it go to waste."

She swallowed back another twist of her stomach. "I don't care much for fish."

"Fine." He started to turn away, then his implacable gaze seemed drill into her again. "You're not on one of those ridiculous diets, are you? You're too damn skinny as it is."

Outrage burned away the last of her nausea. "What I eat or don't eat is none of your concern." She winced as she heard her mother in the haughty words. She'd become so focused on correcting her pattern of using helplessness to get what she wanted, she'd been blindsided by her fallback manipulation—the blue-blooded imperative that had been her birthright.

She wanted to blame Gabe Walker—standing there reading her mind, as if he had a right to her every thought. But responsibility had to fall squarely on her own shoulders.

Taking a breath, she tried again. "I'm sorry, I just…" Energy seemed to seep from her body. She wanted his sympathy, ached for it almost as much as she craved her next drink. That he was so strong, so capable only made keeping to her resolve ten times harder. "It was a long drive. I'm just tired."

His gaze strafed her. "I can see that."

So much for sympathy. "I thought I'd lie down for a bit."

"Good idea." He turned to go.

"Would you mind if I napped by the fire?"

"Don't expect me to tiptoe around in the kitchen."

"Of course not. I just…" She couldn't bear the thought of being alone, the way it sharpened the lonesome ache inside her. Standing on her own two feet didn't mean she had to cut herself off from humanity. She could allow herself that bit of vulnerability. "I'm just a little chilly."

Nodding, he turned away and the tension inside Lori eased a bit. She remembered fat pillows on the sofa and a crocheted afghan. With the fire blazing, that should be sufficient for warmth.

Stacking two of the pillows against the sofa arm, she lay down and pulled the afghan over her. A blower on the woodstove sent heated air toward her, the droning noise a soporific. In moments, her eyes drifted shut.

Why hadn't he cooked the trout? He'd been looking forward to it since he got here—fresh-caught rainbows sautéed in lemon and butter, with a massive baked potato on the side. Instead he'd cleaned the five fish, tossed them in the freezer, then started rummaging around in the kitchen for an alternative dinner choice. Just because trout didn't please Lori Jarret's palate.

Gabe pulled canned corn and peas from the pantry cupboard, then found tomatoes and shell macaroni. He'd discovered a chub of frozen sausage in the freezer and with the loaf of sourdough French he'd brought with him, he could put together a halfway decent meal of soup and bread. With any luck, his fussy housemate might actually like it.

He didn't know why he cared. She was exactly the kind of woman he tried to avoid, the ones with more problems than good sense. Whatever she'd been looking for up here at the lake, he wasn't providing. He was here for his own selfish reasons. He ought to be looking out for himself, not a beautiful woman who could only mean trouble.

Still, a pot of soup sounded pretty good, would take the chill off the rapidly cooling evening. And it was just as easy to cook for two as for one. It wouldn't kill him to share.

Locating a can opener in a kitchen drawer, he looked across the breakfast bar to where she lay on the sofa. He could see only the top of her head, the flames turning her hair to molten gold. When she'd emerged from the bedroom earlier, he'd seen the wash of color on her mouth from a fresh application of lipstick, saw the faint pink of blush on her cheeks. His first impulse was to think she'd put on makeup to catch his attention. But considering her actions since, it seemed she was more interested in hiding than showing off.

As he dumped the veggies into a small Dutch oven, Lori shifted on the sofa, then settled back again with a sigh. There was something about her that made him want to go sit beside her just to watch her sleep. That ticked him off royally. It wasn't so much the perfection of her face and the lines life had placed there—and it was damn near perfect despite the paleness of her skin—as whatever she concealed beneath the surface.

That made her all the more dangerous. He liked his world up-front and straightforward, without hidden agendas. Women like Lori—like his ex-wife, Krista—kept their secrets undercover. By the time a man figured out what they were up to, the worst had happened.

Pulling a skillet from beneath the stovetop, he took the sausage he'd defrosted in the microwave and broke it up into the pan. Before long, the sausage sizzled and popped, the sound loud enough to make him wonder if he'd wake her with the noise. He would have liked that better, having her awake instead of soft and warm and asleep under that afghan. But the woodstove's fan probably muted the sound of cooking because she didn't stir.

The pot of water he'd started for the macaroni hit

the boiling point and he dumped in half the plastic bag. Grabbing a wooden spoon from a basket by the stovetop, he ran it through the pot of water, turning down the electric coil at the same time. The sausage had nearly lost its pink color and once he added it and the pasta to the vegetable base, the soup would be nearly done.

Lori sighed again, one delicate hand stretching up above her head. In spite of himself, he looked for a ring. Her left hand was bare. That didn't mean a damn thing, of course. If she was a married woman away from home she might not wear a ring. There were plenty of reasons a woman might not want to adver-tise her marital status, but if Lori was on the prowl, she didn't seemed inclined to make a play for him.

Again, he tried to match the image of the soused woman he'd given a ride home with the fragile beauty on the sofa. There was always the possibility Lori's inebriation wasn't typical, that it had just been a night with the girls that got out of control. But he recalled the haggardness of Lori's face, the bloodshot eyes that told a tale of too much alcohol far too often.

I'm not doing that anymore. He'd heard enough drunks make that kind of promise. But Lori's tone when she'd told him seemed matter-of-fact, not an avowal. It wasn't his concern if she took another drink or not, but he knew what kind of nightmare path al-coholism could be from the DUIs he'd arrested, not to mention the cops in the LAPD who had chosen that form of distraction from pain.

Draining the macaroni, he poured the contents of the colander into the soup pot. Using a slotted spoon to add the sausage, he turned the burner up a notch to finish heating the soup. He couldn't find a basket for the bread, so he just put the thick slices into a plastic bowl.

One last stir of the soup and he headed out to the great room. Lori had pulled her arm back in again and curled her elbows tightly into her middle. She was sunk so deep in sleep, he half wondered if she'd taken a sleeping pill after he'd left her in the bedroom. Not the best strategy for an alcoholic to go from one addiction to another. Still, it was none of his concern.

He brushed his fingers along her arm, the slightest touch, and she gasped and snatched it away from him. Her brown gaze fixed on him in wild-eyed confusion a moment before she remembered where she was.

He shoved his hands into his pockets. "Dinner's ready."

She took in a deep breath. "You didn't make the fish?"

"Felt like soup. Sausage and canned veggies." He stepped back as she sat up slowly, pushing her hair back from her face. "It isn't much."

"That sounds great." Her voice, still liquid with sleep, trilled along his spine. "Are we eating at the table?"

"I found a couple TV trays stashed in the pantry. Thought I'd eat by the fire."

She smiled. "I'd like that."

She set up the trays while he served up the soup. Then she carried out the bread while he brought the bowls to the great room. She'd arranged the trays on opposite ends of the sofa, about as far apart as they could be. The bread she set between them on the middle cushion, within easy reach.

He watched her eat, took in the almost desperate speed with which she spooned up bites of soup. As she took a slice of French bread to dip in the broth, her hands shook.

Concern welled up inside him, followed closely by irritation. "When the hell did you eat last?"

A flush rose in her cheeks and she set down her spoon. "I had something at breakfast."

Impatience flared. "You can't go all day without eating. You already look like you could blow away in a stiff breeze."

The pink in her cheeks deepened. "I didn't want to take the time during the drive."

"Lady, if you passed out on the road and killed yourself, how long it took to drive here would be pretty moot."

"You're right." She picked up her bread again and swabbed at the soup with it. "I need to eat."

She took a careful bite of bread, then started spooning up the soup again. Her movements seemed intentionally slower, more deliberate. He realized he was still staring at her, a big mistake. He repositioned his tray more toward the fire, slightly away from her, and bent his head to his dinner.

Dabbing up the last of the broth with a final chunk of bread, he pushed back his tray and rose. "There's more if you want it."

Her bowl was still half-full, a crust of bread beside it. She shook her head. "I've had enough." She lifted her water glass and drank deeply.

He left her alone, going to refill his own bowl. As he returned to the great room, she passed him with her dishes, giving him a wide berth. Watching her over the breakfast bar as she rinsed her bowl, glass and spoon, he wondered if she'd go hide in her room once she was done.

But after she'd stowed her dishes in the dishwasher, she came back out to the great room. Tugging the afghan over her, she snuggled on the far end of the sofa.

"So you're a sheriff," she said softly.

"Deputy." He mopped up the broth in the bottom of his soup bowl. "Brent Larkin's still sheriff."

"I remember him, back when…" She looked down at her slender hands interlocked on the lavender afghan.

She didn't seem inclined to finish. He'd never been much for small talk, but he managed to scrape up a conversation starter. "You're from Marbleville?"

"San Francisco. I lived in Hart Valley a few years."

It must have been before he'd arrived six years ago, or he would have recognized her that night at the Two-Step. "Did you live in town?"

"A few miles out. You wouldn't know it." Pushing off the afghan, she reached for his empty dishes. "Let me get these."

He tried to get to them before she did and ended up with his fingers tangled in hers. She froze, head down, a curtain of golden hair hiding her face. "I can get my own dishes," he told her.

"You cooked. I should clean up."

There was no reason to push the point, to keep his hands on hers when he'd sworn he wouldn't touch her. But somehow, following through on his promise was harder than he'd expected.

On her feet, she swept the bowl and glass away before he could protest again. He let her go, not liking his body's reaction to her, the way her warmth still heated his palms.

He followed her into the kitchen, but kept space between them as he tore a couple paper towels from the roll and wet them at the sink. Once he had the trays wiped down and put back in the pantry cupboard, he'd run out of reasons to be around her. For the life of him, he couldn't quite figure out why he wanted to be.

"Coffee?" he asked, turning to the cupboard.

She shut the dishwasher. "Is there decaf?"

A cursory inspection produced only a can of regular. "Sorry. Leaded only."

"Then no."

He pulled the can of coffee from the cupboard. "You might take a look. I know Sadie likes that frou-frou herbal stuff."

From her hesitation, you would have thought he'd asked her if she wanted to run for president. She waited until he moved aside, then made her own foray into the pantry. She unearthed a box from the back.

"Mint. This would be great." She smiled, only the second genuine smile he'd seen on that exquisite face, and he understood every hapless guy who did something stupid for a woman. A woman like Lori, whose face could commute darkness into sunshine. She didn't say another word, but he felt like a slave at her bidding.

She shouldn't have smiled at him. She saw her effect on him, his purely male response to the light in her eyes, the curve of her mouth. She'd seen that reaction too many times. Without any effort, without any real desire to do so, she'd captivated a part of him, the physical part of him. She'd traded on that effortless ability all her life, had cajoled and persuaded with only a smile, gotten exactly what she wanted.

But now she hated it, wished she could tear it from her face. She didn't want Gabe thinking about her, raking her body with his gaze, imagining what lay beneath her jeans and sweater. She wanted to just disappear, vanish into a nonentity. At the least, run to her room and hide.

Which would be easier than accepting herself as she was. Easier than accepting her missteps, the tragedies she'd created, the hurt she'd caused. She didn't want to be beautiful anymore, because she didn't want to be herself.

Lori set the herbal tea on the counter next to the can of coffee Gabe had unearthed. As his coffee brewed in the coffeemaker, she filled the tea kettle and set it on the electric stove. The water heated, the pot rattling on the glowing coils. She felt a little like that kettle, its unseen contents bubbling and roiling toward an explosion.

Why can't life ever be easy? she fretted and a moment later nearly laughed out loud at herself. That had been her problem all along—everyone had wanted to make her life easy. They'd removed every stumbling block, whisked away any difficulties, made sure every ocean she sailed was smooth as glass. She'd never done any heavy lifting, had never strained a muscle, had never worried her pretty little head about anything. The ones who'd most wanted to help her had left her helpless.

Gabe reached up into the cupboard above the breakfast bar and produced two mugs, his lean body an irresistible temptation. Hugh the Rat might have had a prettier face, but he didn't have one tenth the appeal of Gabe Walker. And yet she'd let Hugh talk her into his bed, had been all too ready to accept his avowal of love, his easy promises. When she'd been working so hard on changing herself, she'd fallen into the old trap of trusting everything that came out of a man's mouth, especially when the man was as good-looking as Hugh.

Hugh was gone now, good riddance. He and his pretty face vanished the day she'd delivered the news. After the panic of abandonment had faded, gratitude had swamped Lori when she'd realized she'd dodged a bullet when Hugh had revealed his snakey nature by leaving her in the lurch.

Gabe set a mug on the counter for her, and she tore open the herbal tea packet and dropped it in. The tea kettle started its whistle, screaming into the silence of the kitchen. She grabbed the kettle from the burner and poured boiling water over her tea bag as Gabe served up his own cup of dark, rich coffee. As she inhaled the sharp fragrance, her nerve-endings screamed for the caffeine, but she wouldn't let herself even think about drinking a cup.

Booze, coffee and men. Her own triple threat. She was determined not to fall for any of them.

Gabe drank his coffee straight, exactly how she liked it. His gaze fixed on her as he sipped from the mug. "You going to drink that before it gets cold?"

She looked down at the pallid cup of herbal tea. "Is there honey?"

"Think I saw some way in the back."

She stepped toward the pantry cupboard just as he did. They nearly collided, and Gabe took her shoulders to keep from bumping into her.

"Sorry," he muttered.

She ought to back away, ease away from his touch. But the contact felt too good, and she didn't seem to have the strength to break it. Even as she realized the wrongness of aching for the touch of a total stranger, she couldn't urge her feet to move.

It had been this way with Hugh when she'd met him at a meeting and he'd smiled at her, taken her hand. She'd been weak then, only eight months sober, still finding her way. His touch had melted her.

But she was stronger now. She'd had to struggle for every inch of progress, ought to have muscles like a bodybuilder. That she could so easily grow weak again at a man's touch filled her with despair.

His hands dropped from her shoulders. Grabbing up his coffee mug, he leaned against the sink. "Second shelf from the top, on the right."

It took her a moment to understand what he'd said, then she remembered the honey. Peering inside the open cupboard, she found the sticky bear-shaped plastic bottle and pulled it out.

Leaning against the sink, he sipped at his coffee. "So you live in San Francisco?"

She squeezed a generous dollop of honey into her tea. "Noe Valley."

"Pricey area."

She shrugged. "It's a small apartment."

Her parents owned the complex and it was the one concession she'd been forced to make. Her job at the teen center barely covered food and utilities. If her microscopic salary had had to cover rent as well, she'd be out on the street.

Using her parents' apartment meant she wouldn't have to tap the trust fund for expenses. That knot was far too tight to untangle, too close a tie to her parents. It was as close to living on her own terms as she could manage at the moment.

With the honey added, the tea was sweet and warm and seemed to fill in the empty spaces inside her. "Thanks," she said.

He gave her a puzzled look. "For what?"

"For suggesting the tea." She took another sip. It wasn't the dark, bitter drink she craved, but soothed nonetheless. "It's just right."

He still studied her, and his green eyes seemed to see far too much. "You'd think no one ever did you any favors."

"They've done me far too many." Her gaze dropped to the mug in her hand and she said more softly, "But in the end, they didn't do me any favors at all."

Gabe watched as Lori drank the last of her tea. The woman was such a crazy contradiction, one moment seeming vulnerable and needy, the next as inflexible as steel. It was as if she was a painting in progress, an image the artist couldn't quite decide how to capture, one that changed from moment to moment, reinventing herself with each stroke of the brush.

But always breathtakingly beautiful. It might be rude to stare, but a face like Lori's begged him to drink in every detail, every curve and line captivating and tantalizing. The softness of her eyes, the silky gilded hair, seemed made for a man's admiration. Krista had been a pretty woman and he'd thought he loved her, but Lori's brilliance would have eclipsed Krista into shadow.

Her mug empty, she gestured with it toward him. "Can I use the sink?"

She didn't get any closer, obviously waiting for him to move. Just as well. Despite his determination not to, he didn't trust himself to not give in to the urge to put his hands on her. Much as he'd tried to justify each touch—he'd had to wake her for dinner, they'd both reached for the same dish, they'd nearly bumped into one another by the pantry—he knew he was treading into perilous territory.

Anger welled up—at himself for losing his focus on what was important, at her for being so damned beautiful. These two weeks were about his son, and what his next steps should be. There was no room in his plans for a gorgeous blonde who only meant trouble.

He pushed away from the sink. "Go right ahead." He clenched his teeth to fight back to urge to let her body brush against his.

She kept plenty of space between them. "Thanks."

She took his place at the sink and turned on the water. A quick rinse, then she opened the dishwasher to put the mug inside.

Drying her hands on a kitchen towel, she turned to him. A strand of her hair had fallen forward and he itched to sweep it back over her ear. He longed to do even more than that—caress her face, draw his thumb across the fullness of her lower lip, cover her mouth with his. He thrust the images aside.

She hooked the errant strand behind her ear herself, then stepped around him. "I'm going to bed. I have a long drive tomorrow."

The reminder that she was leaving in the morning teased him with the possibilities. They could have one wild night, then she'd be gone from his life, no strings, no attachments. That he'd even consider such lunacy was proof that it had been too long since he'd gone to bed with a woman.

"See you in the morning, then," he told her as she slipped from the kitchen.

"Probably not." She stopped at her bedroom door. "I plan to get an early start."

The thought of her being gone when he woke set off an uneasy ache inside him. "I'm going into town tomorrow for supplies. I'll follow you in."

She shook her head slowly. "That's not necessary."

"Humor me."

A moment's hesitation, then she nodded. "Fine. I'll wait for you."

She stepped inside her bedroom and closed the door behind her, leaving Gabe to wonder why another hour with this woman meant so much to him.

Chapter Three

Whether it was the quiet, the scent of pine permeating her room or her exhaustion, Lori slept well, waking only when the first light of the sun filtered through the pleated shades on the windows. It was nearly seven-thirty when she left her room dressed in jeans, T-shirt and a soft, well-worn San Francisco Giants sweatshirt, her hair pulled back in a ponytail. She didn't see Gabe in the kitchen or great room and she wondered if he was still asleep.

Then she saw the pan of blueberry muffins out on the counter and the half-empty pot of coffee. The herbal tea was still out on the counter, next to a clean mug. When she lifted the tea kettle, it had been refilled. That surprised her; he'd seemed unwilling to do any more for her than was absolutely required.

Where was he? Had he changed his mind about seeing her off? Maybe he wanted to get an even earlier start than she did and had already gone into town. Turning on the burner under the tea kettle, she went to the front window and checked for his truck. When she saw it still parked there, relief expanded inside her. She might not have wanted to acknowledge it, but if he'd left without saying goodbye, it would have been nearly unbearable. Even if she didn't quite understand why.

She heard the sound of the back door and turned to see him enter with an armload of wood. He nodded in greeting. "Morning."

"Good morning."

She watched him cross to the woodstove and drop the split oak into the andiron beside it. He wore a heavy denim jacket over his T-shirt and Lori caught a glimpse of the Marbleville Sheriff's Department logo when he bent to open the woodstove and add another log. He jabbed at the fire with a poker, sending up sparks.

Stove door shut, he replaced the poker and turned to face her. "I made muffins."

"I saw them. They look great."

He shrugged. "From a mix. Help yourself."

The tea kettle started up its whistling scream and Lori hurried into the kitchen. As she poured the boiling water over the bag of peppermint tea, a sudden longing to stay washed over her. The peace of this place had already crept into her bones and she knew it was exactly what she needed to heal herself, to find her way again.

If only she could take Gabe's place here. It wouldn't be right; he'd had the first invitation. But in that moment the thought of driving back down the mountain seemed intolerable.

With her first sip of honey-sweetened tea, her stomach started sending out warning signals. She knew she had to eat, had to try to get something down, but even Gabe's fragrant muffins seemed to set off a rebellion. Maybe if she drank a little more tea, things would settle down and she could take a few bites.

His jacket off, Gabe entered the kitchen and crossed to the coffeemaker. "Grab a muffin. I can't eat them all."

She struggled to swallow another mouthful of tea. "No, thanks. Maybe I'll take one with me."

His mug filled with coffee, he leaned one hip against the breakfast bar. "I checked your oil."

"You didn't have to."

"Never met a woman who maintained her car properly." He sipped his coffee. "Tire pressure's low on the right rear. Make sure you stop at a service station in town."

"Okay. Thanks." The tea wasn't doing anything to quiet her stomach. She struggled to hold on, to avoid that mad rush to the master bathroom. But as the contents of her stomach tumbled and roiled, she knew it was a lost cause.

"Excuse me," she gasped out before cutting around him and racing for the bedroom. She banged her elbow on the door as she moved past it, the stinging pain only adding to her nausea. She got the bathroom door shut and the toilet seat up in the nick of time.

There wasn't much to lose, just the little bit of tea she'd managed to get down. Pushing back to her feet, she flushed the toilet and rinsed her mouth at the sink. Her contrary stomach, completely empty now, grumbled with hunger.

Maybe she'd try the muffin first this time. Or a handful of crackers, if there were any in the pantry. She could probably pick up a packet when she stopped to put air in her tires.

When she opened the bathroom door, Gabe stood on the other side and she jumped back in surprise. Her heart stuttered in reaction. "What is it? You're ready to go?"

"What's going on?"

"Nothing." Collecting the last of her toiletries, she eased past him into the bedroom. Her no-nonsense flannel nightgown still lay on the bed, and she snatched it up, embarrassed that he might have seen it. She stuffed the gown and the toiletries into her suitcase.

"You looked pretty damn green a minute ago."

Focusing on her suitcase, she zipped it shut. "The tea didn't hit me quite right."

She saw the frank disbelief in his face. "I'll take that," he said, reaching for the Louis Vuitton.

Grabbing the handle herself, she lifted it from the bed, then hooked her purse strap over her shoulder. "I've got it."

"Suit yourself." He left the bedroom, snagging his jacket as he headed for the front door. He held it open for her, then locked it after them. "You remember how to get out of here?"

"The directions are still in the car."

Preceding her down the stairs, he had her trunk popped before she got there. He let her handle the suitcase herself, slamming the trunk lid closed once she'd set it inside.

"You have your cell?"

"In my purse." She'd discovered she'd packed her charger after all, had found it tucked away in the bottom of her suitcase. She'd recharged it overnight.

He unclipped his cell from his belt. "Give me your number." She reeled it off to him and he programmed it into his phone. "Save mine on yours. In case you have trouble getting home."

She pulled out her phone and dutifully went through the steps to save his number in memory. Then she climbed into the Civic and started the engine.

But when she made to shut the door, he stopped her. "Be sure to get that tire filled."

"Right. Thanks for everything."

He nodded, then finally stepped aside so she could shut the door. She started the engine, backed around his pickup then pulled out onto the drive. She waited until his truck was behind her before she continued along to the asphalt easement road.

In the daylight, traversing the road's curves was easier than it had been yesterday near dusk. The sky arched overhead a brilliant blue, and only the mildest breeze teased the sapling pines and cedars. It was the kind of day that should have lifted her spirits, filled her with contentment. Instead a lead weight seemed to lodge inside her.

I don't want to leave. The realization hit her hard as she pulled out onto the main highway into town. She'd given herself this gift of time, had allowed herself the luxury of escaping her life for two weeks to put into perspective her situation, the decisions she had to make. Having to leave so quickly made her feel a bit resentful.

She wanted to blame the feeling on the man following behind her. That was her usual modus operandi, to make something or someone outside herself responsible for her emotions. If she did that, she could rely on that someone to fix the problem, to make it better. It was so much easier that way.

I don't want to leave him. That was even crazier. She barely knew him. The few hours they'd spent together had painted a picture of strength and confident power, exactly the kind of man she fell for so easily. Yet, when she'd met Hugh, his arrogance and inflated ego had come across as strength at first, and he'd seemed so ready to take charge of her life. That he was so different a man at the core only pointed up her inability to discern true character.

They hit a straightaway with towering ponderosas on either side and Lori accelerated. Few houses were visible along this stretch of highway and traffic was light. The commercial area lay just ahead where she and Gabe would part company. She felt a pang inside, anticipating that moment when she would pull into a service station and he would drive on by, maybe saluting her with one last farewell wave.

She'd only glanced in the rearview mirror a split second, had only taken her attention off the road for that brief duration. The deer had leaped seemingly from out of nowhere, suddenly scrambling onto the roadway in the path of her Civic. Lori had only time to register the size of the buck, the dull brown hide, the antlers branching on its head.

She swerved in reaction as the deer leaped to safety and disappeared. But suddenly a semi loomed large in her windshield, hurtling toward her, its horn blasting. For a numb moment she wondered why the huge truck was traveling the wrong way in her lane. Then she grasped that she'd swerved into oncoming traffic to avoid the deer. The massive semi nearly on her, she wrenched the wheel back to the right, and prayed her car would turn in time.

* * *

As the disaster unfolded, Gabe watched in helpless horror, his vision narrowing on that small silver car, the deer leaping past. Time slowed to a crawl as Lori veered into the eastbound lane and the semi bore down on her. His hands gripping his own wheel so tight he could feel the laces of the cover digging into his palms, he willed her to turn away, to pull the car to safety.

When she did, her quick maneuver sent her sedan careening across the roadway onto the shoulder. It skidded and fishtailed in the dirt, the car's tires hitting a soft spot that sent it spinning in a half circle. The back door of the driver's side of the silver Honda slammed into a towering ponderosa, the car finally coming to a rest with its front end partway on the pavement, facing the wrong way.

Pulling right up to her front bumper, he slapped on his flashers, grateful he'd been following her. Someone else might have been driving too close, could have collided with her car. He didn't like to think what might have happened to her in a secondary collision.

Scrambling from his pickup, he hurried over to the driver's side door of Lori's car. She sat with her hands over her face, the airbag pooled in her lap, her breathing coming in rapid gasps.

He opened her door, did a cursory scan for obvious injury. "Take it easy. You keep breathing like that you'll pass out."

Dropping her hands, she looked up at him, her eyes huge in her face. "I didn't see it. I couldn't… It just jumped…"

Her whole body shook convulsively and he wondered if she was going into shock. "Did you hit your head?" he asked, probing with his fingers.

"No." She fumbled with her seat belt, managed to get it off, then shoved aside the airbag. She immediately flattened her palm over her abdomen, pressing lightly. "I think I'm okay."

"Where's your phone? I'm calling the EMTs."

"I can't afford…" Her hand on her abdomen clenched. "You're right. We should call them." She dug her phone out of her purse.

The truck driver had pulled his rig over. He trotted across the road toward them. "Is the lady all right?"

"Think so." Gabe dialed 911.

As Gabe spoke to the Highway Patrol, the truck driver scribbled on the back of a business card and handed it to Lori. She slipped it into her purse.

The truck driver returned to his truck. As the semi pulled out, drivers in both directions slowed to look their fill at the accident.

Assured the ambulance was on its way, Gabe hung up. "You have any flares?"

With a trembling hand, she reached for the trunk release. "Not sure. Let me look."

She turned in her seat and made a halfhearted effort to get up, but he put a hand on her shoulder. "I've got some in the truck."

Slamming her trunk shut again, he retrieved two flares and set them, burning, in the roadway. That wouldn't stop the "look-e-loos," but at least there was clear warning of the accident scene.

When he returned to Lori's car, she was hunched over, her head between her knees. A memory intruded—Lori in the back of his patrol car, drunk, vomiting. His stomach sank and he half expected to see an open bottle on the seat beside her before he came to his senses. She hadn't been drinking; this was just a reaction to the accident.

She sat up and gave him a wan smile. "I thought I was going to lose it for a second there."

A silky strand of hair had slipped from her ponytail and he gave in to the impulse to sweep it back. Her brown gaze locked with his as his fingers grazed her ear and he could see her pulse race. It took an effort to pull his hand away, to break the connection with that smile.

"I'll call for a tow." He backed away from the Honda.

It had been bad enough at the chalet, keeping his distance when she was so close. But in the aftermath of the accident, when she was so vulnerable, it seemed as if all his good sense had been stripped away.

Opening the passenger side of the truck cab, he reached into the center console for his cell. As he shut the console, he spied Brandon's photo where he'd taped it to the dash. The last picture he'd ever taken of his son, he'd found it in the throwaway camera a week or so after Brandon was gone.

The sweet three-year-old face grinned at him, the dark hair spiky with cowlicks, the green eyes full of mischief. If nothing else could ground him, wake him up to the crazy line he was treading with Lori, his son's memory could. This was why he'd come to Tahoe—not to meet a woman or indulge his physical needs. He'd agreed to the two-week retreat to come to terms with the absence of his son.

Kissing his fingertips, he pressed them lightly to the photograph, the familiar ache tugging at him. Then he straightened from the truck, and dialed his auto club.

* * *

"A week?" Lori stared at the manager of the body shop, unbelieving.

Jim, the beefy man behind the counter, shrugged in apology. "We have to requisition the door panel and airbag from Sacramento. They're on strike back east and everything's on back order."

Lori had known she wouldn't be heading home that day. But a week? "You can't just pound out the dents?"

The manager smirked in Gabe's direction. "Can't send you off without an airbag, lady. That tree did a number on your car."

Tears of frustration threatened. It had all been too much—the accident, the jostling ride to the emergency room in the back of the ambulance then the long wait for a doctor. Gabe was at her side every moment, a comfort and unnerving distraction all at once.

Gabe had left the room when the internist had finally arrived, wasn't there when she haltingly related her concerns. When the doctor examined her and told her everything was fine, the intense relief had nearly brought her to tears.

Darned if she'd cry now in front of heartless Jim. She tilted up her chin. "How long to install the airbags?"

"Two or three days. Maybe hubby will let you drive his pickup in the meantime." Jim chortled. "If he trusts you behind the wheel."

Gabe edged forward. "Just do the work, Jim. And keep your mouth shut."

Gabe didn't raise his voice, didn't bluster. He

didn't need to. Jim's grin vanished and he nodded. "Yes, sir. I'll give you a call when the work's done."

With a firm hand on her back, Gabe escorted her from the body shop's office to where the tow driver had left her car. "Pop the trunk," Gabe told her. "I'll get your suitcase."

Once she'd pulled the release, she dug around for the books that had been scattered under the seats when she'd hit the tree. She felt a little light-headed when she straightened with the stack and had to lean against the car for a moment before she headed toward Gabe's pickup.

During the drive with him from the hospital to the auto body shop, she'd still been caught up in the aftermath of the accident and emergency room visit. She'd been able to close him out, to shield herself from him out of self-preservation. But with the trauma of the crash easing, her focus had shifted unerringly back to him. How would she fight that sizzling awareness of him in the close quarters of the truck cab?

He waited by the open passenger door and helped her up into the cab, his touch impersonal. She set the books at her feet, the top one face-down so the title wouldn't be obvious. Then as she angled to find the seat belt, he reached across her toward the dash. He pulled something off the vinyl above the radio, then slipped it into his jacket pocket.

She considered asking, but before she could frame the question, he'd shut her door and started around the front of the truck. He climbed into the driver's seat and put the keys into the ignition. "Where to?"

The truck had bucket seats rather than a bench and she was grateful for the console separating them. Still so frazzled by the encounter with the deer, she wanted nothing more than to move closer to him, have the comfort of his touch, his warmth.

She linked her hands in her lap. "A rental car place, I guess." How she'd pay for it, she had no idea. She had one credit card with a minuscule limit. If not for her car insurance, repairing the car would have been out of the question.

"You're going home?" he asked.

"What else would I do?"

"Stay in a hotel."

She shook her head. A local motel would cost even more than a rental car. "Maybe there's bus service to San Francisco."

"You're not staying at the chalet." Now he sounded angry.

"You had prior claim."

He looked ready to pull the steering wheel from its column. "I'm not leaving."

"I didn't ask you to."

"Just because I let you stay at the place one night doesn't mean we could do it for two weeks."

Two weeks with Gabe Walker. The thought both thrilled and terrified her. "We can't stay together."

He glanced at her across the console, turbulent emotions in his green gaze. "It's ridiculous."

"What is?"

"To drive all that way. Turn around and come back."

"I told you. I can't afford a motel." She tipped her chin up, determined not to feel embarrassment. There was no shame being of limited means, even if she hadn't been raised that way.

"Don't stay at a motel." The words sounded as strangled as the steering wheel in his hands. "Stay at the chalet. With me."

Was he possessed? Completely unhinged? What in hell prompted him to abandon common sense and make such a crazy offer?

Not to mention she immediately assumed he was making some kind of proposition; he could see it in her face. The accusatory look in her eyes, the trace of color flushing her cheeks—she thought he had designs on her.

Not that he was completely guiltless. His intentions in extending the invitation might have been altruistic, but there was no denying the erotic notion or two featuring Lori Jarret he'd entertained during the night. That internal X-rated movie had been harmless enough when he thought she'd be exiting his life soon, but now it came back to bite him in the butt, tempting him with possibilities.

He refused to go there, slammed a lid on even the suggestion of intimacy with the slender woman beside him. Whatever ulterior motive had simmered in the back of his mind about her, he'd bury it deep. He'd had plenty of practice burying emotions.

"Stay the week until your Civic is repaired. I think we can stay out of each other's way."

"It would be better if I didn't." Her exhaustion weighted every word.

"I'll have my hands full with repairs to the chalet. Every minute I'm not working, I'll be dropping a fishing line in the lake. We likely won't even see each other."

A part of him prayed she'd say no, leave him to his isolation and persistent grief. The photo tucked in his pocket was what really mattered these next two weeks.

But then she smiled and he thought his heart would stop. "I enjoyed dinner together."

The remembered pleasure of sharing a meal with her seeped into him. Ruthlessly, he pushed aside the softness. "Cooking dinner for you won't be part of the plan."

She flushed and turned away. "Of course not."

Was she doing this on purpose? Yanking him one way and then the other? That had always been Krista's modus operandi. Could be Lori was just as manipulative, whatever her story.

"We'll see how it plays out." He twisted the key in the ignition and the truck's engine roared to life. "You're staying, then."

"Sure. It makes sense."

He backed the truck from its parking slot and pulled out of the lot. "I only got enough grub for me. I didn't notice any groceries in your car yesterday."

"I'd planned to go shopping today."

He heard the tremor in her voice and as he braked the pickup at a red light, he turned to her. The color had drained from her face and she looked ready to pass out.

He resisted the urge to take her hand. "What's going on?"

The light changed and the idiot behind him honked an instant later. With a growl, Gabe wrenched the truck around the corner and pulled into the parking lot of a strip mall. Killing the engine, he gave in to his impulse. Her hand felt cold as ice.

"You feel sick? Talk to me."

"Light-headed. Woozy. Think I should have eaten."

"No kidding." He took a quick glance around, spotted a deli a couple doors down. "Put your head between your knees. I'll be right back."

As he trotted over to the deli, he tried to calculate what would be easy on her stomach, but provide a quick jolt of calories. Maybe crackers to start, then some cheese for protein.

It crossed his mind she could be pretending to be nauseous, using it to get him to respond to her. But on the heels of that cynical thought he realized her pallor would have been difficult to fake. And she'd already had him, hadn't she? He'd agreed to let her stay.

In the deli, he grabbed some saltines from a shelf as he headed for the front counter, spying the dairy case on his way. A bottle of orange juice looked like a good bet and he added that to the string cheese and crackers. He was back out at the truck in less than three minutes, trying to ignore the fact that he felt like her lackey.

She straightened as he climbed in. She'd regained a bit of color, but looked transparent with hunger.

Tearing open the crackers, he handed her a thick stack. "Probably reaction to the accident coupled with an empty stomach."

"Probably." Downing the saltines in quick succession, she took the OJ and gulped down half the bottle. She took a breath, then took the unwrapped cheese from him. "Thanks."

She smiled again, her eyes shy, her mouth gently curved. There was something about that sweet gesture that made him want to move the world for her.

Had he ever felt that way about Krista? Even at the beginning, when he'd felt so certain of his love for his ex-wife, long before she'd cut out his soul, he didn't remember an emotion even close to what Lori seemed to stir in him.

But he didn't feel anything for Lori, not really. Her desperate situation had just touched something inside him, that part of him, nearly buried, that still couldn't resist helping someone in need. Once she got her car back and headed down the road, he'd forget those soft brown eyes, that heart-stopping smile.

He pulled the remaining string cheese from the plastic bag. "Want another?"

She shook her head. "I'm fine, thanks. Much better."

"Good. We'll head for the Safeway and do our shopping."

Taking the bag from him, she folded shut the top of the crackers and put them and the empty orange juice container into the bag. "You do this a lot, I guess," she said as he started the truck again.

He directed the pickup back onto the street. "Do what?"

"Help people."

He shrugged. "It's part of my job."

She sighed, a lonely sound. "Most times I can't even help myself."

There wasn't a shred of self-pity in the words. They were a simple statement of fact that despite his resolve to keep his distance, pushed him to probe deeper.

But he wouldn't. If he had any hope of remaining neutral the next few days sharing the chalet with Lori, he'd best know as little about her as possible. What he knew already was far too much.

Chapter Four

Gabe held the bagged chicken out to her, his stern expression more than a little intimidating. "We can share it."

"It costs too much." The six-pack of drumsticks she'd picked out was half the price of his choice. Not to mention she had no idea how to cook a whole chicken. Drumsticks she could nuke in the microwave.

He put the plastic bag in the cart. "Then I'll pay for it."

"I pay my own way." She removed the roaster and set it back in the refrigerator case.

He looked ready to put it back in the cart and she entertained a brief, ridiculous image in her mind of them playing keep-away with the bag of chicken.

Hands pressed on the metal edge of the cart, he leaned toward her. "Two bananas, a minuscule bunch of broccoli, the smallest loaf of bread the store sells—are you on some kind of nutty diet?"

The only diet she was on was of the money variety. She had a limited budget for this trip and Gabe's choices threatened to blow all of it in one shopping trip.

There was more in the cart than the three items Gabe had listed—small packages of lunch meat and cheese, canned soup—not the hearty, ready-made brand Gabe had suggested, but the less expensive condensed variety. She planned to add milk and orange juice when they reached the dairy section.

By now, Gabe was no doubt heartily regretting his offer to let her stay. Nevertheless she had to stand her ground. "I know how much I eat. It makes no sense to get more than I can use."

He just stalked off, leaving her to follow. Her sights on the dairy section at the other side of the store, she made the giant mistake of letting her attention drift, her gaze fixing on the contents of a familiar aisle.

She stalled out, freezing in her tracks. Up ahead, Gabe must have sensed she no longer followed him, because he turned toward her. As bad as it was to fight this battle when she shopped alone, it was completely mortifying in front of a witness. You would have thought after thirteen months of sobriety she could pass by the liquor aisle without stopping.

But there she stood, her hands gripping the cart to keep herself from that habitual stroll along the rows and rows of colorful glass bottles of whiskey, wine and beer. For some alcoholics, it was getting past the entrance to a bar, for others, being in the company of others drinking. For her, the supermarket aisle filled with endless options for oblivion screamed out a siren call she hadn't yet learned to completely ignore.

Gabe had returned to the cart, standing quietly as she willed herself to walk past. When she gathered the courage to look his way, relief washed over her at what she didn't see in his face—judgment, pity. There was no support either; he certainly wasn't rooting for her to make the right choice. His expression was neutral. But what could she expect from a total stranger?

In the end, she pushed past, keeping her focus on the dairy case. Grabbing quart cartons of orange juice and milk, she detoured up the soft drink and chips aisle to get to checkout. The chips were easy to ignore, the tempting array of caffeine-laden colas less so. They had been a daily staple in her diet when she'd first quit drinking, the Coke without the rum, the 7-Up without the Seagram's. Eventually, she'd recognized them as the crutch they were and forced herself to give them up. In her current condition, they were forbidden anyway.

At the checkout stand, Lori counted out her precious twenties, then put her hand out for the change. Gabe scooped up the four plastic bags before she could even get her wallet back in her purse. The constant tension between them, the stress of the accident, her changing body's demands all combined to drag the last shred of energy from her. She just wanted to get back to the chalet and collapse in the master bedroom.

In the truck, she leaned back against the seat and shut her eyes. "We should trade," she said softly as he pulled out of the parking lot.

"What?" The irritation was still apparent in his tone.

"You should have the master bedroom." She could barely get the words out. "I can take the smaller room."

"You'd have to use the bathroom across the hall."

"That's not a problem."

"It's a problem to me."

She opened her eyes and sat up. "I don't mind—"

"No."

"But—"

"It'd be more of a pain in the butt to move my stuff again." His jaw flexed. "Stay the hell where you are."

"If you want me to go home—"

"Drop it."

"I can see it's an imposition—"

"Drop it, Lori." He bit the words out as he stopped at a red light.

Inexplicable tears tightened her throat and she raised a hand to rub her eyes. She could feel his too-observant gaze on her before the light turned green and he started through the intersection. But if he expected an explanation from her, he would be disappointed. Her emotions had become untrustworthy, slippery things these past several weeks. She barely understood them herself.

She'd never felt this way the first time, with Jessie. Back then, she'd cut herself off from the booze, cold turkey, just after she'd realized she was pregnant. She hadn't had the months of sobriety beforehand, the serenity of working the program. She'd been so on edge, she'd felt almost nothing for nine months but the constant craving.

Reflexively, her mind tried to close itself off from thoughts of Jessie, walling itself from the pain. But that was part of the purpose of these two weeks of isolation and introspection. Reconciling the mistakes, making amends for the pain she'd caused others. She owed the greatest debt to her daughter and could no more ignore that obligation than she could numb it with alcohol.

Jessie's face swam into view, the sweet smile she'd had at age four, before... Grief snagged her unexpectedly and her eyes filled in earnest. She thought the tightness in her throat would choke her. There was no hiding the wetness spilling down her cheeks.

"Tissues are in the glove box."

She didn't dare turn toward him. Fumbling open the latch, she groped in the glove box for the small plastic packet of tissues. She dabbed at her face, grateful she hadn't bothered with makeup that morning.

"Thanks." Her voice barely shook. She waited for his questions.

But he just drove on in silence, the rhythm of tires on pavement soothing, easing away the pain.

At the chalet, he carried in her suitcase and two bags of groceries, leaving her only the books to bring inside. He'd barely dropped the other two bags in the kitchen before he headed out again, back into town to complete his aborted trip to the local hardware store.

She watched him drive away through the living room window, waiting for the familiar sense of aloneness to wash over her. She didn't know how to be alone; that had always been part of her problem, what she'd tried to numb with drinking. But it was testimony to the strength she'd built up in the past several months that she felt only the slightest twinge of fear when Gabe disappeared around the first curve of the drive.

As she put away the groceries, her gaze fell on the cell phone she'd left by her purse. She'd already checked in with her sponsor this morning. She'd had to keep her call brief because Amy had to get to work to prepare for a court case she was adjudicating that day.

Amy had suggested they hook up later that day when she recessed court for lunch. Lori wished they could talk now, that she could tell Amy about her struggle on the liquor aisle, her loneliness, her exhaustion.

And about Gabe. But what would she say? He was exactly the kind of man she'd fought giving in to, yet at the same time was nothing like any of the men she'd let herself fall prey to. She realized it wasn't so much who Gabe was that was problematic, but who *she* was when she was with him.

Better not to mention him at all to Amy. She and Gabe would be together only for the week or so it would take to get her car back. They had agreed to keep their distance from one another, allow each other their space. She wouldn't fall into the same trap with him as she had with other men.

A moment's hesitation, then Lori picked up the cell. There was another call she had to make, one she ached for, yet dreaded. She hadn't phoned Jessie in nearly two weeks despite her vow to speak to her daughter at least weekly. She loved her daughter so much, yearned to hear her voice. But impenetrable walls lay between them, barriers she didn't know how to breach.

Barricades Jessie had every right to erect.

Lori's thumb passed over the three on the keypad, the speed dial she'd set up for the Double J Ranch. Her daughter's face floated in her mind's eye, not the eleven-year-old she was today, but the sweet four-year-old she'd once been, before Lori's mistake had ruined her daughter's life.

Guilt ate at her, urged her to shove the phone back in her purse. She clutched it tighter, then nearly dropped it when it burbled in her hand.

Caller ID displayed a cell number, then Gabe's name. She pressed the answer button. "Hello?"

"I figured I'd pick up a sub sandwich for later," he said without preamble. "Do you want one?"

His voice sounded far too good to her. Phone against her ear, she just wanted him to keep talking, to take away her pain inside.

"No, I'll just make something here." She searched for something else to say, a way to keep the link between them. "Thanks anyway."

"I'll be another hour or two."

"See you then."

He disconnected and she hung up her own phone. Tucking it into her purse, she decided she'd call Jessie later, when she wasn't so exhausted and feeling so vulnerable.

When Gabe was here. As much as she might want to deny it, his presence gave her a strength she hadn't quite been able to muster while she was alone. It wasn't because he meant anything to her personally. She barely knew the man. It was simply that she still needed the company of others, no matter how determined she was to stand on her own two feet.

There was no shame in that.

It was testimony to how much Lori Jarret had rattled him when he nearly broke down by the playsets.

The local hardware store hadn't had everything he

needed for the deck and plumbing repairs, so he'd headed for the larger store up the road for the lumber and pipe fittings the smaller store hadn't carried. When he headed outside to the lumber department for the redwood two-by-sixes, he passed a sturdy wood play set that had been constructed by the exit.

It was nearly identical to the one he'd bought for Brandon ten years ago. The kit had included the same tire swings, climbing ropes and striped canvas cover over the top of the plastic slide. He'd just started putting it together, he and Brandon working to inventory the parts. Brandon would look at the picture of a nut or bolt, then dig through the packages of hardware to find a match.

Is this it, Daddy? Is this the right one?

It shouldn't still hurt this much. After ten years, the pain ought to have faded. He should be able to think of his son and not feel his heart breaking all over again.

His hand fell to the cell phone on his belt and he had it unclipped before the impulse reached his consciousness. Against all logic, he wanted to call her, for her comfort, to simply hear her soft voice. Lori Jarret was a stranger to him and far too needy, far too vulnerable despite the iron strength he sensed under the surface. He certainly shouldn't be relying on her for reassurance.

Resolutely, he clipped the phone back on his belt and continued past the redwood playset. He quickly located the lumber he needed and found a flatbed cart to load it up on. Keeping his gaze straight ahead as he pulled the cart past the play set, he made a few more stops for the odds and ends he still needed, then headed for the checkout. His purchases safely in the bed of his truck, he nosed the pickup over to the sub shop at the other end of the center housing the hardware store.

She'd said she didn't want a sandwich, but he found himself ordering one for her nonetheless. If she didn't like the small turkey and cheese sub, he'd just have it as a snack later, maybe this afternoon after he'd put a few hours into the deck repair. It would keep well enough in the refrigerator.

At the register, he asked for two cookies, one peanut butter, one chocolate chip. Odds were, she'd like one of them.

When he carried the bag from the shop, he felt a little foolish having bought a sandwich and cookie for a woman he'd insisted he wouldn't give any special treatment. But it wasn't as if he went out of his way here. He'd planned to get himself a sub; why not buy her one too, just in case?

As he drove from the parking lot, he swore he wouldn't do a damn thing more for her.

On the back deck in a chaise lounge she'd found in a storage shed behind the house, Lori heard the crunch of gravel that signaled Gabe's return. She'd lain there for the past hour or so, snuggled under the afghan she'd brought out to ward off the chill, flipping through one of the books she'd brought with her. She kept the packet of crackers at hand as well in case her nausea returned, and for the first time in a long time, her unreliable stomach hadn't given her any trouble.

The front door slammed and she heard the creak

of Gabe's steps across the living room. Slipping her book under the afghan, she rose, then bent to pick up the crackers. A sudden wave of dizziness washed over her and she sat back down on the chaise lounge to let it pass.

High altitude and low blood pressure were a bad combination. Feeling her light-headedness ease, she took a breath and got to her feet again. The dizziness returned with a vengeance and she stumbled as she stepped toward the back door.

"What the hell?" Strong arms caught her before she sagged to the deck. In another moment, the world spun as he lifted her and carried her back inside. She should have been embarrassed, but his firm, warm chest pressed against her felt so good.

"I'm sorry," she said as he set her on the sofa.

"If you tell me you haven't eaten, I swear—"

"I ate." She eased herself up, feeling too exposed lying there on the sofa. Her dizziness had receded. "A muffin and some juice. And I've been munching crackers all morning."

"Then why were you about to pass out?"

"I have low blood pressure." That was certainly true, although she didn't bother to tell him why. "I just stood up too fast."

His hard gaze fixed on her and she could see him searching for the lie in her face. He bent closer and for a moment, she had the crazy idea that he might kiss her. But she heard him sniff, and her cheeks warmed when she realized what he was doing.

"I haven't been drinking," she told him, making certain there was not the least trace of self-righteous indignation in her tone.

He straightened. "I brought back a sandwich for you."

"I told you I didn't—"

"Don't eat it if you don't want it. It's in the fridge."

He headed out the front door. Getting slowly to her feet, she gave herself plenty of time to steady herself before she followed him out front.

He had the tailgate to the truck down and was carrying a load of wood up the stairs. He set the pile of lumber on the deck, then returned for the rest.

"Can I help?" she called down the stairs to him.

He looked ready to say no, then surprised her when he nodded toward the plastic bags still in the truck bed. "You could bring those up. They're not too heavy."

She descended the stairs, edging aside as he started up them with the last of the wood. Testing the weight of the bags, she picked the lightest two. She didn't want to take any chances lifting something too heavy.

At the foot of the stairs, she shifted both bags into one hand, wanting to keep a hand on the stair rail. As he passed her on the stairs again, she tried to squeeze herself aside, but her arm brushed his. Heat radiated from the point of contact.

She set the bags of hardware beside the lumber. "What all do you have to do?"

He ascended the stairs with the last of the bags. "The deck has dry rot here and there. Have to pull out the bad wood and replace it with new. Then there's the plumbing work inside."

As he sorted through the bags, she leaned against the deck rail, well clear of him. "How is it you know so much about fixing things?"

"Worked in construction just out of high school, then summers during college. Took me a while to figure out what I wanted to do."

At least he had. She was still working on that one. "Have you known Tyrell a long time?"

"Close to twenty years." He dumped the contents of a bag onto the deck.

It crossed Lori's mind that she and Gabe might have both attended Ty's and Sadie's wedding. She had only a vague memory of the event eight years ago. That had been before Jessie's accident, when she drank to hide a different kind of pain.

She decided she'd rather not know if Gabe had been there. "Were you with the LAPD as well?"

He looked at her over his shoulder. "I realize this is just a vacation for you, but I've got work to do. Could you leave me to it?"

"Sorry." She pushed off from the rail and walked away from him, along the wraparound deck toward the rear of the chalet. "I'll be out back."

She doubted it mattered to him where she went as long as she wasn't with him. She couldn't blame him. He'd planned on having the place to himself and here she was, pestering him. It wasn't his fault aloneness was such a struggle for her.

Picking the afghan up from the chaise lounge, she reached for the book, then set both down again. The lake beyond beckoned, and although it terrified a part of her to go off on her own, Sadie had told her the trail was well-marked. She'd just retrieve her cell. Better to have it with her for safety's sake.

She stepped inside, praying she wouldn't encounter Gabe before she could slip out again. Once she had the phone in her jeans pocket and hurried outside, she quietly descended the back steps.

A few moments later she found the trailhead near the shed and was about to head down when she realized the day had finally warmed enough to make her sweatshirt unnecessary. Tugging it off, she left it on a nearby tree stump before taking her first careful steps down the trail.

His rudeness was uncalled for. She'd just been trying to make a little conversation, being polite. It wasn't her fault he couldn't control his response to her when she was nearby.

But it was just as well she'd left. He'd be pulling the power tools out of his truck pretty soon and the last thing he needed was to be distracted with a circular saw in his hands. He liked having all ten fingers attached.

Still, he could have been a bit more politic. He could have said, *Hey, I really have to focus on my work here,* or *How about we talk at lunch?* But in that moment he'd been damn near desperate to get that sweet, tantalizing voice out of earshot. He'd thought he could shut her out by keeping his back to her. But then she spoke and he couldn't think of anything else but how her body had felt for those few brief moments in his arms.

Picking her up had seemed like the right thing to do at the time when she'd pretty much swooned into his arms. It had been no more than a few moments before he set her down again, but the feel of her still lingered. The swell of her hips, the firmness of her thighs, the soft pressure of her breasts against his chest.

He'd been an idiot to touch her at all. But if he hadn't grabbed her, if she'd slammed her head on the deck… He couldn't let her hurt herself.

It had made him sick to think she might be drinking again. He'd had more than one friend who'd given up the booze, had sworn to stay sober, then fallen into temptation again. He never felt good about it, but his reaction to the possibility that Lori might have fallen off the wagon hit hard. Because she was a woman, maybe, or because she seemed as tortured by demons as he was. Not because she mattered to him.

He had the odds and ends sorted out—lumber, deck screws, power drill and bits—and arrayed across the deck. The pipe fittings, plumber's tape and wrench he had by the door, ready to take inside. The circular saw was still in the truck and he needed to grab the sawhorses Tyrell had told him were stored in the shed out back.

Now would be a good time to retrieve them. He still had to inventory the bad spots on the deck, wasn't quite ready to start cutting. But he might as well have the sawhorses handy.

Of course, he could check on Lori while he was at it. Not that he needed to keep tabs on her, but she had nearly taken a header a few minutes ago. It wouldn't hurt to make sure she was okay.

He'd go for the sawhorses first since that was his real reason for going out back. Then he'd use the back stairs to carry them up onto the deck, could give Lori a once-over before getting back to work.

He knew he wanted to give her more than a once-over. He wanted to join her on that chaise lounge, pull her into his lap, touch her everywhere. Carrying her those few feet into the house he'd gotten only a taste and he hungered for so much more.

Shaking off the images of Lori's skin against his, he double-timed it down the stairs and trotted toward the shed. The small structure was a miniature twin to the house, its wood siding stained the same rich color as the chalet. He slid open the doors and waited a moment for his eyes to adjust to the dim interior. As he stood there, his gaze strayed to the trailhead just beyond. Something black and orange sat on the tree stump that marked the start of the trail.

Unease prickled up his spine. He crossed to the stump and lifted the sweatshirt from it. Lori's. She'd been wearing it this morning. An unreasonable panic sparked inside him.

Calm down, he told himself. *She's up on the deck, right where she said she'd be.*

She must have taken the shirt off when she got out the chaise lounge, left it here by mistake. But no, she'd been wearing it when he'd returned from the hardware store. Could she have taken it off up on the deck, hung it over the rail and a wind caught it? But the air had been still all morning.

Fear clutched at him, a terror he didn't even understand. He ran for the stairs, calling out, "Lori!" When she didn't answer, when it was obvious she wasn't in the chaise lounge, his terror ratcheted up another notch. Tossing aside the sweatshirt, he yanked open the door, ran through the house, checking every room. She wasn't there.

Back outside, he reached for the sweatshirt he'd discarded on the deck. As he clutched it to him, a memory intruded, sharp and painful. Brandon's small sweater on his empty bed. Him racing through the house in L.A., scouring every room for a trace of his son. Coming up empty.

He dragged in a breath, fighting to calm himself. This wasn't Brandon missing all over again. Lori was probably fine. He just needed to give himself a moment to think and he'd figure out where she was.

The trail. She'd gone to take a walk down to the lake. Without telling him she was leaving, without informing him where she was going. Irritation tugged at him, replacing the crazy fear. Dropping the sweatshirt on the chaise lounge, he trotted down the stairs and back to the trailhead.

Chapter Five

The broad boulder overlooking the lake still held the morning chill and Lori regretted leaving her sweatshirt above. She could have spread it on the granite surface for padding and insulation from the cold. As it was, even her heavy denims didn't shield her from the icy stone.

Nevertheless, the jewel-blue water spread out before her filled her with a serenity she thought at times she could never achieve. The faintest breeze ruffled the needles on the ponderosas, the impossibly blue sky mirroring the deep sapphire of the lake. She could hear the occasional motorboat in the distance, but this private little cove seemed cut off from the troublesome world she'd left behind.

A motorboat roared past, this one close, intruding on her peace. She shivered in the shade of the pine trees and decided next time she'd come down here with a blanket to spread over the rock and her sweatshirt tied around her waist. It crossed her mind that if Gabe had been with her, she could have snuggled up to him, let the heat of his body ward off the chill.

Wrong train of thought. Gabe had made it pretty

clear he didn't want her around. In any case, she was here to learn to be alone, not take up with yet another man.

She slid down the side of the boulder, taking care to settle herself before starting up the trail again. Her earlier light-headedness had caught her off guard. Her blood pressure had always been on the low side and her earlier pregnancy had exacerbated it, just as this one had. She'd just have to be more careful.

She hadn't climbed far before she had to stop to catch her breath and she realized ruefully she was really in no shape for this kind of exercise. Her short walks from her Noe Valley apartment to the nearest BART station didn't exactly prepare her for mountain hiking. She'd just have to take it slow up the hill.

Another motorboat passed by in the distance and it wasn't until its raspy engine faded that she heard the scrape of footsteps from above. Although it was possible that one of the Kings' neighbors could have taken this path down to the lake, it wasn't likely.

Lori's heart, already laboring over the climb, accelerated as she anticipated Gabe's arrival. Her gaze on the cluster of trees that shielded the last turn of the path just above her, she felt ridiculously giddy. She might try to put it down to the thin mountain air, but she'd be lying.

He skidded down the last few feet before he reached her side. His face looked a little wild, his green eyes lit with fire. Without a word, he grabbed her shoulders, his hands hot through the thin knit of her T-shirt. His grip tightened and his sharp gaze roamed her face, settled on her mouth.

* * *

He didn't know how he would keep from kissing her. Her lips had parted in surprise, her brown eyes had softened as if in expectation. If he didn't hammer some quick sense into his head, he'd do something incredibly stupid.

He forced himself to focus on the irritation he'd felt when he realized she'd left without telling him. He gave her an angry shake. "You don't leave without telling me."

"I just went for a walk."

"You were alone. Anything could have happened."

She tried to twist away from him, but he held fast. "I brought my cell. I could have called you. For that matter, you could have called me."

Now he felt like a complete dunce. It hadn't even crossed his mind to try her cell. He dropped his hands and stepped back.

"You're right." Agitated, he raked his fingers through his hair. "Sorry."

"I should have told you I was going."

"Yeah. Just so I know." He looked up the hill, loath to leave her. "I have to get back to work."

"I was on my way up anyway." She smiled. "I'm afraid my lungs aren't up to the task of climbing."

After her smile, he barely comprehended what she was saying. Her smile pretty much wiped his mind clean.

"I can give you a hand."

Which was exactly the wrong thing to do, because it involved touching her again. Nevertheless, he took her arm. As he urged her up the twists of the trail, he kept his mind strictly focused on the task at hand instead of the feel of her skin. It didn't help that her faint scent teased him, a fresh floral fragrance in her hair tempting him with possibilities.

They had to stop several times along the way to let her catch her breath. He could let go of her then, could tear his gaze away from her chest rising and falling as she filled her lungs then let out the breath on a sigh. The sound drove him crazy, passed over his body like a caress. At one point, he was almost afraid to take her hand again for fear he would pull her close, give in to the impulse to kiss her.

He never would have thought hiking was an erotic experience, but by the time they reached the top of the hill, he was ready for a cold shower. How he was going to safely do his work after close contact with Lori, he had no idea.

She pulled away from him and it took everything in him not to bring her closer again, especially when she hit him with another smile.

A strand of golden hair had come loose from her ponytail and she swept it behind her ear. "I'm going to lie down for a few minutes."

"I'll be running the power saw pretty soon."

"I brought earplugs. In any case, I don't want to sleep as much as just rest."

The picture of Lori stretched out on that king-size bed lodged itself in his mind, impossible to shake loose. "It'll be a few minutes before I turn it on. Still have to check for all the spots that need repair."

She edged away. "See you later then."

Resolutely, Gabe turned back to the shed and the sawhorses inside. He'd just reached for them when her sweet voice tugged him around again.

"Thanks for helping me up the hill."

"Sure."

She hurried toward the steps then, and he watched her climb to the deck, then retrieve her things from the chaise lounge. He didn't move a muscle until she'd entered the house and was out of sight.

She didn't fall asleep, not then with Gabe working just beyond her bedroom, not later that night after an afternoon and evening spent in a delicate dance pretending they weren't acutely aware of one another. She'd been smart enough to resist going out to the kitchen when she heard him come in from lunch, had stayed in the bedroom going through the motions of reading one of her books. After he'd finished and gone back to work, she'd gone out to fashion her own lunch from what she'd bought at the market. The sub he'd bought for her, its fat French roll tempting, she left in the refrigerator, instead eating the pallid sandwich she'd slapped together.

She wasn't as lucky that night in avoiding him, was only halfway though her microwave meal when he emerged from the shower, sandy hair slicked back, the clean scent of him tantalizing. She'd gulped down her meal too fast, then paid for her folly when her stomach rebelled and she nearly lost the few calories of nutrition she'd managed to get down.

Too fidgety to hide away in her room, she'd gone out on the deck to watch the sun sink into the trees, its brilliant light limning the trees with flaming coral and deep red. The mosquitoes drove her back inside where Gabe ate his solitary meal at the breakfast bar, an outdoorsy magazine spread open by his plate. She'd wanted nothing more than to move up behind him and rest her cheek against his back. Instead she escaped to her room.

Where she should have been tired enough to sleep. But she lay there, every step he took in the great room strumming on her nerves, edgy as she listened for Gabe's every move. She'd stuffed earplugs in her ears, but though they muted the sounds of his feet treading back and forth past her door, her overstimulated mind filled in any missing details. Her eyes were closed, but she saw him nonetheless. Not even the television, which he turned on thirty minutes or so after she lay down, could keep her any more awake than her own imagination.

She finally fell asleep long after he'd gone to bed, then slept until nearly ten when Gabe's saw woke her. She'd managed a bowl of cereal for breakfast, felt ready to kill for the last cup of coffee Gabe had left in the pot, then spent the remainder of the restless morning on the sofa in the great room, flipping through a book she barely absorbed.

When the saw fell silent again, she checked the clock. It was close enough to noon to have lunch. Her stomach was just starting to send out its first queasy warnings; better to eat something before the nausea appeared full force.

Setting aside the book, she got up carefully, then headed for her bathroom to wash up. When she stepped out into the great room, Gabe was in the kitchen. He had a massive sandwich on a paper plate, some canned peaches and chips beside it.

"There are more peaches." He set his plate on the breakfast bar, then put a can of cola beside it. "That sandwich is still in the fridge."

She'd managed to resist temptation yesterday, but her stomach's imperative sapped her determination. She had to eat, and now.

She found the paper-wrapped sandwich and the half-filled can of peaches and quickly served them onto a plate. She stared longingly at the four cans of store-brand cola next to her milk carton, then resolutely took out the milk. She took her plate and filled glass over to the breakfast counter.

Nudging the bar stool aside to get some space between them, she sat next to him. She had to force herself to eat the sandwich slowly, knowing her stomach might object otherwise.

She'd wolfed half of it down before setting it on her plate to take a drink of milk. "Thanks so much."

He shrugged in acknowledgment. "I'll be using the saw all afternoon. I hope you weren't expecting quiet time."

"I have some reading to do." And her journal. She'd been too restive to pick it up since she'd gotten here. "I'll just go out on the back deck."

"I'll be replacing deck all over. It'd be quieter reading in the bedroom."

She bit back her irritation. "I'd rather be outside."

He gulped down soda, then slammed down the can. "I can't stop working just so you can commune with nature."

"I didn't ask you to." Her cell phone started up its burbling and she snatched up her purse. "Do whatever you want."

As she scrambled to find her phone, he ate his last bite of sandwich and washed it down with soda. The caller ID displayed Amy's number and relief lit inside her. If she ever needed her sponsor it was now.

"Hey, Amy," she said with a smile.

In the process of tossing his trash under the sink, Gabe's gaze locked with hers. He was angry at her, that was clear enough, although she didn't understand why. The rest of what she saw in his green eyes sent a jolt of awareness through her.

She turned away, tried to focus on what Amy had just said. "Sorry, I didn't hear that."

"Just asking how you're feeling," Amy repeated.

She risked another look up at Gabe. He was still watching her, his shoulders taut with tension. "I'm fine," she said, the words coming out breathless.

Gabe shut the cupboard door and strode out of the kitchen. "I'll be outside." The front door closing behind him resounded through the empty house.

Lori's silent prayer that Amy hadn't heard his voice went unanswered. "Who is that?" There was no judgment in Amy's tone, just cautiousness.

"His name is Gabe. And there is nothing," Lori said before Amy could intervene, "*nothing* between us." Lori quickly related the details of the mix-up with Sadie's and Tyrell's invitations, the car accident, her agreement to stay. She omitted any mention of the powerful attraction she felt for Gabe. That was nothing more than her usual habitual response to a man.

Amy remained quiet for several moments after Lori finished. "You know I'd come get you. You only have to ask."

"I also know your crazy schedule. I won't have you

moving court dates just to give me a ride home. And I'd just have to come back in a few days."

The saw started up outside, its harsh roar as impossible to ignore as the man wielding it. With an effort, Lori returned her attention to Amy. "I wanted this time," she told her sponsor. "The situation isn't ideal, but I'll be fine."

"Have you called Jessie?"

Lori squeezed her eyes shut as guilt pierced her. "Not yet."

"How long has it been?"

"Too long. I'll call when I hang up with you."

Lori heard voices in the background, then Amy had to say a quick goodbye. Lori had no choice but to follow through on her promise.

She pressed the three on the cell's keypad, then lifted the phone to her ear. As the phone at her ex-husband's house rang, once, twice, three times, she sent off a silent cowardly plea that no one would answer, that she could leave a message for her daughter on the machine. But just as the recorded greeting started, it cut off.

A soft female voice said breathlessly, "Hello?"

Lori recognized the woman as Andrea, Tom's wife. Andrea was unfailingly polite whenever Lori called, but Lori could never quite forget the first time they'd met. She'd been drunk and rude and cruel and Andrea had every reason to despise Lori. Yet she didn't, in fact went out of her way to demonstrate her forgiveness for Lori's efforts two years ago to tear her and Tom apart. Lori had to struggle not to feel ashamed whenever she spoke to Tom's sweet wife.

"It's Lori. Is Jessie there?"

"She's over at Sabrina's today. I can have her call you when she gets home. I know she'll want to talk to you."

But she wouldn't. Their conversations were awkward and stilted. "I can call back. When will she be home?"

She heard Tom's voice in the background asking, "Who is it?" Just as Andrea answered him, the chalet's front door opened and Gabe stepped inside. He headed for the kitchen and pulled open the fridge.

"Andrea?"

But Andrea didn't answer. In another moment, Tom came on the line. "What do you want?"

Gabe pulled out a cola and snapped it open. He took a long drink, seeming in no hurry to go back outside.

Lori fought to keep her tone even. "I want to talk to Jessie."

"It just upsets her. She doesn't know if she can trust you. She's afraid you'll just leave her again."

Emotion tightened her throat. "I know. But I have to try."

Quiet ticked away. She could feel Gabe's steady gaze on her. Finally Tom said, "I'll let her know you called." He hung up and Lori disconnected her phone, feeling wrung out.

Gabe set his can down on the counter and turned to wash his hands at the sink. "Broke a tooth on the saw blade. I'm going back into town to pick up another. Did you need anything?"

She couldn't help herself; she glanced up at the liquor cabinet above the wet bar. That would ease the pain inside, soothe the guilt. But it wasn't a choice for her anymore.

"Can you give me a minute?" she asked, reaching for the phone book on the counter. She flipped through the yellow pages, her finger running down the As. Dialing the number she found, she sagged in relief when someone answered.

She glanced at the clock. There was an afternoon meeting at a local church. She'd be late, but better to go than stay here alone.

Dropping her cell phone back in her purse, she turned to Gabe. "Could you drop me at the First Baptist Church along the way?"

He glanced down at the phone book, and she could see him take in the page heading. "Sure. I'll pick you up on the way back."

"Thanks." She grabbed her sweatshirt and purse and waited until he'd locked the back door.

Out on the front deck, he unplugged the circular saw and removed the blade, then set it in the toolbox mounted in the bed of the truck. She waited for him in the cab as he shut the tailgate.

When he slid behind the wheel, she let out a breath she didn't even realize she'd been holding. "How long do you think you'll be at the church?"

"The meeting should be over by two-thirty."

He didn't ask what meeting, didn't have to. He started the truck and pulled out, his quiet presence a comfort precisely because he didn't offer any.

The church sat beside a park just outside of town, and when he pulled up to it, his gaze strayed to the playground next door. Two young girls sat at the top of the jungle gym while a broad-hipped woman pushed a smaller boy on the swings. Gabe fixed his gaze on the boy, his green eyes bleak with pain.

Lori touched his arm. "What is it?"

He tugged away. "I have to get going."

She climbed from the truck cab and shut the door. He wouldn't look at her as she watched him through the window. Redirecting her thoughts toward the meeting she'd come for, she went inside the church.

The ache around his heart never went away. In the ten years since he'd last seen his son, the agony had faded to a more bearable pain, one he could handle day to day. He prided himself on his ability to perform normally, as if he hadn't had the guts ripped out of him a decade ago.

But suddenly everything felt as fresh as that day when Brandon first disappeared. He could blame it on his solitude at the chalet, or the most recent disappointment in the search for his son. But he didn't like lying to himself.

It was Lori Jarret. She'd managed to fracture the surface of ice he'd encased around his heart, made him feel again, if only a little. Not so much because he felt anything for her, but because she'd set his world off-kilter. He didn't like it, wanted back the numbness he'd carefully cultivated over the years.

Emotion wouldn't get his son back. Feelings wouldn't find him. Strong leads and sure, accurate information would. They'd been in short supply lately, cooling an already cold trail, in return building another layer around his heart. Lori Jarret had no right to invade that protection.

Despite his mental order not to, his gaze strayed

to the boy arcing back and forth on the swing. He looked nothing like Brandon—his eyes and hair nearly black where Brandon's eyes were green and his hair a shade lighter than Gabe's own sandy brown. He was a bit older, too, beginning to lose the babyish look Brandon's face had still held at age three. Yet the sight of that boy on the swing, his childish face lit with a brilliant smile, chipped away at the ice inside.

Savagely, Gabe wrenched the truck into gear and gunned it from the church parking lot. A glance in the rearview mirror told him he'd caught the attention of the young mother. She probably thought he was some kind of perv watching her son. Thank God she wouldn't likely be there when he got back.

He kept his mind as blank as he could as he returned to the hardware store for the saw blade. While he was there, he picked up another package of deck screws, the mundane task an opportunity to dull the edges the boy in the park had honed to painful sharpness. He took another several minutes deliberating in the electrical aisle, searching for wire to connect the small television in his room with the satellite system the other two house TVs used.

When a sales associate wandered up to ask if he needed help, Gabe engaged the man in a weighty discussion of the best way to run the television cable—in the attic or through the crawl space under the house. Then they laboriously searched for the proper fittings and a crimping tool to install them.

Anything to keep from thinking about the boy, about Lori, about his own son. After years of narrowing his focus on the search for his son instead of the fact of his being missing, Lori had somehow shaken his single-mindedness, opening himself up to the fresh terror and agony he'd felt ten years ago. He was shutting the door on those memories again. Now.

His hardware purchases complete, he dropped the blade and cable off in the truck and walked catty-corner to the drugstore in the same strip mall. A headache pounded in the base of his skull and he hadn't had the foresight to bring any pain reliever. Stepping inside, he brusquely questioned a clerk, then headed for the aisle he needed.

In the back of the store, he could see the big packages of baby diapers stacked on the shelves. He wouldn't look at them, wouldn't even think about them. He refused to let that image of his infant son into his mind; that was a sure path to hell.

Clutching the bottle of pain reliever, he nearly race-walked to the checkout, memories crowding in. He felt like he was in some kind of mental meltdown, a frightening maelstrom of emotion. He'd damn well better get a grip or he'd end up driving his truck into a tree just like Lori had.

He gulped down three tablets dry, then dragged in a breath. He hadn't felt so battered since the night he'd searched that empty house. That it had come from out of nowhere—from just seeing a boy on a swing—made it all the more baffling.

Feeling more settled, he started the truck and pulled slowly from the parking lot. He realized how much he was looking forward to seeing Lori again, just to have her near, have her sitting quietly beside him in the truck. That was all wrong. He struggled to squelch that warmth inside.

Instead of rushing back to the church, he stopped

at the fishing tackle shop he'd passed along the way. He wandered the store, trying to generate interest in the contents of the shelves. He picked up a few lures at random and some premade flies, despite the fact he hadn't brought his fly rod.

By the time he headed back to the truck, he thought he had himself together. The headache had eased, helped along by the bottle of water he'd unearthed from the storage compartment behind the seat. It ought to be time to pick up Lori.

The woman and her children had mercifully left the park. Lori wasn't outside waiting for him, so he stepped inside, loath to move farther than the doors. Adversity brought some people closer to God. He wasn't one of those people.

A young man sat at a table just outside a closed set of doors that probably led to the worship area. Gabe approached. "How long before the meeting's over?"

"A few more minutes." The young man smiled as he chomped his gum. "You can go on in if you'd like."

"Is it an open meeting?"

"Naw."

"I'll wait, then."

He lingered back by the entrance doors, his idle gaze taking in the church bulletins and announcements on the corkboard by the office. A brief glance at the children's drawings posted on one wall and he looked away quickly. He'd finally gotten his mind back on track. He wasn't letting it stray again.

The inner doors opened and people trickled out in twos and threes. Lori was in the middle of the pack, speaking to an older woman who looked as if she could be somebody's grandma.

Then Lori's gaze met his and his world rocked on its foundation. She didn't even give him her knock-out smile, her expression serene, but reserved. But he seemed to have no protection against her, felt stripped bare by a need for her that made no sense.

"Let's go," he told her harshly when she reached his side. He was being rude again, but he felt desperate to put some distance between them. Even as he wanted her closer.

The older woman gave him a fishy look and he could almost read her mind. Men who talked to women the way he'd spoken to Lori sometimes used more than words to keep their women in line.

He forced himself to smile, although the gesture probably looked ghastly on his face. "I've got to get back," he said evenly. "Still have a lot to do."

Lori shook the woman's hand and they exited the church. When she was finally beside him in the truck, some of his tension eased. He didn't want to feel better with her here with him, but he couldn't seem to help himself.

"Good meeting?" he asked, not wanting to pull away just yet.

"It helped." She stared out the windshield as the last of the attendees dispersed to their various cars. "Do you believe in atonement? Forgiveness?"

He wouldn't think about all the things he needed forgiveness for. "I'm not much on the religious stuff."

"I'm not talking about God or religion. I'm talking about people." She turned to him, her brown eyes troubled. "Are there some wrongs that can never be forgiven?"

The memories hitting him with the force of a

sledgehammer, he thought of his son, of the empty house. "Yes," he said in a bare whisper. "Some wrongs are beyond forgiveness."

Chapter Six

Some wrongs are beyond forgiveness.

It shouldn't hurt so much. It was only what she'd thought herself. What clear-eyed Hilde had told her at the meeting, although not quite as bluntly.

What if she can't forgive you? Hilde had said in her faint German accent. *You must accept that she may not.*

Lori thought she was on her way to making peace with that. Then she saw Gabe in the narthex and her serenity seemed to scatter.

They drove in silence back to the chalet, Lori wishing she could reach out to Gabe, just have a moment's contact. Instead she took herself back to the meeting, pulled together the tatters of the peace she'd found there. To her surprise, she found it again, discovered the strength was inside her after all.

She still wanted to touch Gabe. The sound of his breathing, barely audible over the purr of the engine, sifted into her ears, the quietness of it tugging at her attention with each exhalation. His capable hands resting on the wheel, the muscles in his arms working as he turned onto the drive to the chalet, his thigh flexing as he braked then eased onto the gas. Like a breeze ruffling the surface of the lake, his presence scudded along her skin, sensitizing her.

It was just an old habit, she told herself. Men. Their scent, the feel of their warm, hair-roughened skin against her palm. The way their eyes watched her with intense, devouring interest.

Except no man had ever looked at her the way Gabe had. No man had ever given her their total focus, complete attention. No man had ever made her want…what? She couldn't even name the yearning Gabe set off.

They pulled up to the chalet and Lori slid from the truck. Her journal was first priority; she had a tangle of emotions to sort out and she'd do it best on that lined paper. She'd grab a banana as a snack and sit out on the back deck.

But when the journal lay open on her lap as she sat Indian-style on the chaise lounge, her mind was as blank as the page. She felt like a hopelessly starry-eyed teen, itching to write Gabe's name all across the page. She'd never done that as a girl—had already started drinking by high school and the four years were pretty much a blur. But right then, she understood the adolescent impulse.

Then she'd write about him. Frankly, clearly. Put the fragmented emotions on paper.

Gabe makes me feel safe. She scanned the words penned in the neat cursive Mrs. Yates had drummed into her in fourth grade. She wrote on. *But I need to feel that safety inside myself, not from him.*

She heard his footsteps then and her thoughts froze inside her. He came around from the other side of the house, a pry bar in his hand. "I need to pull up some boards back here."

She gestured with the pen. "Go ahead."

There was no way she could write about him with him ten feet away. She circled her thoughts around to Jessie. That was what this afternoon had been about anyway.

She flipped to a fresh page. It would be beyond mortifying if Gabe chanced to see his name inscribed there. Pen poised, she waited for the words to spill out.

But they wouldn't come. She stared down at the open journal, the thoughts and feelings logjammed in the pit of her stomach, as if she'd swallowed them to keep from thinking them at all.

The creak of a board pried from the deck pulled her attention from the empty page. Gabe's powerful hands seemed to reach down inside her, wrench those words lodged deep inside her, forcing them into the open. She felt them in the back of her throat, in her eyes where they burned and teared. They finally escaped from her pen.

I don't know if she loves me anymore.

Gabe tossed aside the broken piece of lumber, and she could almost imagine her heart clattering across the deck, discarded the same way.

She doesn't need me anymore. I think she wishes I would disappear.

Gabe turned his focus on another board, levering under it, wrenching it loose. Pulling it from its moorings.

Maybe that would be best.

The squeal of nails pried loose. The rattle of wood on wood. Another hole opened in the deck. In her heart.

Gabe leaned the pry bar against the side of the chalet. "Stay clear of here. I don't want you falling."

She barely absorbed his warning. She felt cold inside, despite the afternoon's warmth. Gabe walked away, around to the front.

Could I walk away for good? If that was what she wanted?

Dig deep, Hilde had said. Find what's truly in your heart. Except she'd barely scratched the surface and she already hurt so much she struggled against the urge to weep.

I think, she wrote, a tear falling and blurring the ink, *I will always have something to give her, something no one else can give.*

She stared down at the open journal, one or two words nearly obscured by moisture, and prayed that it was true.

Gabe returned to the back deck with several lengths of wood he'd cut to fit the pieces destroyed by dry rot. As much as he tried not to look her way, his gaze strayed to her slender form on the chaise as he dropped the pieces on the deck. She turned her face away from him, and he suspected she was wiping away the tears she'd tried to conceal.

None of his business. He doubled back to the front deck and gathered up his electric drill and extension cord. Tyrell had had several outdoor power outlets installed along the deck, making Gabe's job that much easier.

She'd pulled herself together by the time he returned, the book she'd been writing in shut on her lap, her gaze fixed on the lake. Going down on one knee to switch to a Phillips bit, he tilted his head up just enough to watch her. Even her profile riveted him— her skin the color of rich cream, her mouth impossibly soft, the whorls of her ear where she'd swept back her hair delicate and perfect.

Tightening the Phillips bit, he wondered how she would taste at that pulse point of her throat, how her mouth would feel against his. It seemed he'd developed a pretty vivid imagination when it came to Lori, the sound of her sighs, the feel of her skin against his hand incredibly real in his mind.

Which was exactly where they would stay. A little harmless fantasy was one thing. He wasn't about to act on that lunacy.

Or so he kept telling himself.

His jeans suddenly seemed tight and he stood to release the pressure. Turning his back on Lori, he busied himself with matching cut pieces of redwood with the empty space they would replace.

"I'll be making some noise," he told her as he fit the first piece into the deck.

"That's okay."

Her breathy voice was like a touch along his spine. He bent his head to his work, ignoring the sensations.

Crouching again, he reached out for the deck screws then stared stupidly at the empty space where he'd expected them to be. His mind racing a million miles a minute over Lori, he'd clean forgotten to bring the box around. With a huff of impatience, he went to retrieve them. If he weren't careful, he'd be driving a deck screw into his foot instead of the lengths of redwood.

She was gone when he returned with the screws,

along with the afghan and her books. Okay, that was better. Without her as a distraction, maybe he could get his mind wrapped around his work.

No such luck. She popped back out of the house with a glass of juice and moved to lean against the rail as she sipped the drink. Resolute, he hunkered down on the deck, chin tucked to his chest so he'd be focused on the drill instead of her.

A handful of screws in his mouth, he drove the first one into the replacement piece. The feel of the metal screws in his mouth generated an old memory— three-year-old Brandon beside him, soberly handing him nails as Gabe hammered together a birdhouse. Brandon had wanted to put the nails in his own mouth, but Gabe had explained only grown-ups could do that. Gabe had worried that his son would try it on his own and choke on a nail. He had no way of knowing the real peril to Brandon was his own mother.

He got the last deck screw firmly seated and tested the piece for stability. He'd been about to pat himself on the back for completely shutting Lori out of his mind when a pair of sneakered feet planted themselves in front of him and completely derailed his mental processes.

He had to look up at her. It was only polite. "Yeah?"

Mercifully, her smile was just a gentle curve of her mouth. That didn't send his fantasies rampaging nearly as badly. "I'm going in for some more juice. Can I get you something to drink?"

He wanted to drink from her mouth, taste the tartness of the orange juice, the honey of her tongue against his. Not what she was asking. He framed a rational response. "A soda would be great."

When she walked away, he swore he wouldn't watch her go. He caught only a glimpse of her derriere when he couldn't quite resist glancing up at her before she stepped inside.

He had the next piece in place before she returned, the excuse of the screws in his mouth to confine his conversation to a mumbled, "Thanks," when she set down the cola. He didn't sneak even the briefest glance this time when she walked away.

He didn't have to. Her image was indelibly burned into his brain.

"How long have you been with the Marbleville sheriff's department?"

The screw he'd been about to drive slipped and gouged a track in the redwood. He set it back into place. "Six years."

"Where were you before that?"

He waited until he had the screw seated before answering. He took another from his mouth. "LAPD."

"Is that where you met Tyrell?"

"Before that. High school." He took the last screw from his mouth. "We graduated the same year. Attended the academy together."

"I went to college. Several." She laughed. "Never finished any, though."

That surprised him. She seemed bright and had an Ivy League look about her. "Why not?"

"Let's just say there were too many bottles in the way." She moved closer and lowered herself to the deck. "I'd hoped to start at City College in the fall."

Tightening the last screw, he took the soda can and popped the top. He guzzled down a long swig. "So why not go?"

She looked away. "Something came up. I'm not sure how I can make school work."

"Plenty of student loans out there. And the community colleges are still pretty cheap."

"It's not the money." She laughed again, the husky sound entrancing. "Well, it is the money, but…let's just say there are a few unexpected obstacles."

Only one, really, Lori acknowledged. One enormous roadblock. It was part of the equation she'd come up here to solve, although the answer wasn't any more evident than it had been when she'd arrived.

His throat worked as he took another drink and her fingers itched to test the feel of that strong column. She shook off the temptation.

He grabbed a handful of screws and set the ends in his mouth. "Have a major in mind?" he asked around the mouthful.

"Counseling." She watched him drive a screw expertly into the wood. "Aren't you afraid you'll swallow one of those?"

As he glanced up at her, something flickered in his face, a brief agony. Then he looked down again. "No."

His jaw looked so rigid, it could have been carved from granite. She ached to touch him, to try to ease that tension.

Pushing to her feet, she grabbed the orange juice she'd left on the deck railing. "I'm going to take a walk. Just up to the highway and back." If she didn't get away from him, she didn't know what she'd do. Whatever she did, it wouldn't be smart.

She wondered if maybe he'd tell her she shouldn't

go alone. Maybe even offer to go with her, despite his being in the middle of repairing the deck. A childish part of her longed to have him with her.

But all he said was, "Take your cell," his focus scarcely leaving his work.

"Sure. See you later."

As she passed through the kitchen, she grabbed the phone from the breakfast bar and what was left of a packet of crackers from the cupboard. Out the front door, she hurried down the steps, swinging her arms as she quickened her pace on the driveway.

A short, brisk walk was exactly what she needed. Clear away the confusion, the persistent anxiety that made her vulnerable to Gabe. There was a core of strength inside her; the past thirteen months of sobriety had taught her that. She simply had to tap into it.

As she reached the easement road where the driveway ended, she drew in a breath, the scent of pine translating to a sharp taste on her tongue. Her jumbled thoughts seemed to settle, releasing some of the tightness between her shoulders.

He hurts too.

The thought thrust itself, unbidden, into her consciousness. The image of his face, pain sharp in his eyes, lingered in her mind. An answering ache squeezed her own heart.

She didn't know why, but the realization of his hurt comforted her even as she longed to soothe that pain. That in itself seemed a giant step forward— she'd spent a lifetime cajoling others into helping her. It stunned her to think she had the capacity to help another.

She had to laugh at herself. All the time she'd been

at the teen center, it had always seemed so selfish because she loved the work and adored the kids. It hadn't crossed her mind *she* was helping *them*.

But to help Gabe—that meant getting closer to him. Getting closer threatened to entangle her in the kind of emotional ties that had always led her to disaster. The teens she worked with, despite their troubled lives, responded to her with an uncomplicated love. No strings, no conditions. Gabe represented nothing but strings.

She'd nearly reached the last curve that led to the highway and she slowed her steps. A little winded, she leaned against a tree to catch her breath. Occasionally, the hum of tires on pavement sifted through the trees as a car passed on the nearby highway.

She was here to resolve her own situation. If Gabe chose to open up to her, she could be a sounding board, a sympathetic ear, but it couldn't go any further than that.

She had her own heart to protect.

Maybe he ought to check on her.

She'd been gone maybe forty-five minutes, plenty of time to walk the two-mile round trip to and from the highway. Gabe had finished installing the new deck pieces on the back deck and was nearly done cutting lumber for the few bad spots he'd found on the north side of the house. He hadn't pulled those pieces yet. Once he cut the last of the wood for the next part of the repair, it would be as good a time as any to take a break.

Slapping sawdust from his jeans, he peered along the drive for any sign of her returning. No footsteps on the gravel drive, no golden-blond head appearing through the trees. If she was on her way back, he didn't see her yet.

Worry over her safety nagged at him, distracted him enough that he cut too much off the final length of redwood. He glared at the short piece in exasperation, realizing he'd have to either piece that section like a jigsaw puzzle or cut another length of redwood. Since he'd been pretty miserly buying the lumber, he might have to go back for more.

Better to just go look for her, put his mind at ease, then get back to work. There were maybe a couple hours of daylight remaining, and he still wanted to dunk a line in the lake.

Setting aside the saw, he descended the stairs and started down the drive. He didn't know what was worse—his preoccupation with her when she was near or when she was out of sight.

Not far from where the driveway ended, he caught sight of her down on one knee at the side of the road, her hand outstretched. He slowed, then stopped as he got near enough to see what she was doing. She had a cracker in her hand and was bribing a squirrel with it.

The late afternoon sun sifted through the trees and gilded her hair, the caress of light on her cheek making his heart ache. God, she was beautiful. Even in a lavender T-shirt and jeans, she was like a miracle distilled into the female form.

There was something sweet and childlike about her coaxing the squirrel toward her. A sudden powerful image hit him—Brandon beside her, holding out a bit of cracker in his small hand as Lori encouraged him quietly.

They'd never met and that little boy was gone anyway. Why he'd juxtaposed the two in his mind he didn't understand. Nor did he comprehend why the picture of the two of them together didn't fill him with pain as he would have expected.

Without meaning to, he shifted on the pavement and the sleek gray squirrel, inches from the cracker, spotted him. The critter froze, then when a car approached, it scrambled into the woods.

Lori rose, stepping out of the way of the car and waving to the occupants. When she spotted him, her lips parted in surprise, her gaze fixing on him. Then she busied herself with replacing the cracker in the packet in her other hand and stuffing the plastic wad into her pocket.

"Sorry."

"Just as well." She ambled toward him, her steps as graceful as a dancer's. "I really shouldn't be feeding them, I suppose. I just couldn't resist."

"You'll only encourage them to beg."

"I know." She smiled and he had to steel himself against his immediate reaction. "He was just so cute."

"You know how many diseases squirrels carry?"

"No, and I don't want to know." She continued on along the road. "Are you finished so soon?"

"Taking a break." To find you. But he wouldn't tell her that.

She yawned. "I hate feeling so lazy, but I think I need another nap."

He imagined her stretched out on her bed, then too easily saw himself beside her. "I'll be making noise for another half hour or so, then I'm heading down to the lake."

"I'll take a shower first, then."

That generated an even more erotic image. Her under the shower's spray, water sheeting off her perfect, slender body, her hands soaping her breasts, her belly, her—

He cut off the images rolling in his mind and put on speed up the driveway. "I'd better get to it, then." He trotted to the steps, then hurried up them. As he gathered up the two-by-sixes he'd cut to carry them to the north side of the chalet, he made a concerted effort not to look back at her. He waited until he was sure she was inside the house before he went back to recut the last piece. He took extra care to do it right the second time around.

When he circled back to the north side and dropped the lumber to the deck, the sound of the shower running held him thunderstruck for several moments before he could shake himself back to work. He made enough noise as he could prying up the boards and driving screws into the new pieces. But nothing could drown the beat of running water on the other side of that wall.

Lori felt rested and relaxed when she stepped into the kitchen after her nap. She'd woken to the familiar nausea, but thanks to the crackers she'd left by the bed, her stomach had settled. Now, with any luck, she'd figure out something edible for dinner. Always a challenge, since her culinary skills were limited to scrambled eggs and anything heated in the microwave.

She supposed she could slap together a sandwich. Not an appealing prospect, but even she couldn't mess up a ham sandwich. Or maybe nuke one of the budget frozen dinners she'd picked up, although the meals always tasted more like the plastic container they came in rather than real food.

The back door rattled and she tensed in anticipation of seeing Gabe. He glanced at her as he entered, a shock of awareness streaking through her. He made straight for the sink and turned on the water.

He kept his back to her as he washed his hands then splashed water on his face. His T-shirt taut across his back as he bent to the sink, the play of muscles snagged her gaze. She longed to move up behind him, wrap her arms around his waist, press her cheek to his back.

Her one-track thoughts were on a disaster course again. She angled away from him, leaning against the breakfast bar. Her arms crossed over her middle to give them something better to do, she cast about for something to say. "You didn't catch anything today?"

"Threw back what I caught." He groped for a paper towel. Lori stepped close enough to tear a sheet off for him, then took care not to let her fingers brush his. "No point in keeping fish I won't eat."

Wiping his face dry, he turned toward her. His sandy hair, barely long enough to touch his ears, was damp around his temples, and she wanted to thread her fingers through it. She could cradle his face in her hands, tip her mouth up to him…

He said something, the words buzzing in her ears, bursting the fantasy bubble she'd built. She shook her head. "What was that?"

"Were you about to fix yourself dinner?" He tossed the paper towel under the sink. "I can wait until you're done to start mine."

In her mind, she ran through her options again and decided a budget dinner would be quickest. "I was just planning to have a microwave meal." Her stomach protested the choice. "I'll be out of here in just a sec."

His gaze narrowed on her. "That's not much of a dinner."

She shrugged. "It'll do."

He sighed, glanced out the kitchen window, then back at her. "I'm making spaghetti. If you'll give me a hand, we can share."

She intended to refuse, had the word "no" ready. She'd remind him they were both free agents, that he shouldn't be cooking dinner for her. Not to mention the kitchen was of modest size; if they worked side-by-side they would be too close, wouldn't be able to avoid brushing against one another. She had only to say thanks, but no thanks.

But the words never came. The attraction of sharing a meal with him, taking part in its preparation—never mind that she had zero kitchen skills—was just too strong.

"I'd be glad to help. Just tell me what to do."

He turned away before she could smile. That was one loaded gun he'd rather not face. Instead, he busied himself with pulling ground beef and salad fixings from the refrigerator, then digging in the cupboard for cans of tomatoes and tomato paste. He went back to the fridge for the onion he'd forgotten and handed it out to her.

She fumbled it and it dropped, rolling across the floor toward the cupboards. They both went for it, her hand covering his as he wrapped his fingers around the onion's papery skin. She didn't move right away, which was just fine with him. As much as he told himself it was a bad idea to touch her, his body never seemed to get the message.

Finally, she pulled her hand away and sat back on her heels. "Sorry."

He straightened. "No problem." Turning to the sink, he blasted cold water over the onion to wash it. She was still crouched on the floor. "You okay?"

"Fine. I just..." She grabbed the edge of the cabinet, using it as support as she rose slowly. Almost immediately she tipped, swooning.

He grabbed her before she got far, hands around her upper arms. She slumped against him, her mouth against his collarbone.

"This can't keep happening." He could feel that mouth move as she spoke. "It's ridiculous."

He had to smile at her imperious tone. Despite the blue-blooded look she had about her, the haughtiness seemed completely out of character.

"The altitude can do that to you sometimes, especially if you already have low blood pressure."

She pushed back from him, keeping a hold of his shoulders for support. "I don't think this is good." Now her voice wavered and he saw real fear in her eyes.

He tugged one hand from his shoulder and pressed his fingertips to her wrist. He could see the steady pulsing in her throat, found it far too fascinating to watch it throb. He dragged his gaze to her wrist instead, counting the beats.

"Seventy-two," he told her. "Normal for a woman. How do you feel?"

"Better." She shifted, as if to pull away, but she didn't move an inch. "I think…" The words came out on a sigh.

One hand lay nestled in his, the other hand still rested against his shoulder. No effort at all to tug her even closer, to wrap his arms around her. He could drop a hand to the small of her back, urge her hips against his.

Every bit of sense had fled his brain and he could think of nothing but her mouth, how it would feel against his, the taste of it, the warm moistness. How he would slide his tongue against hers, dive inside, stroke the tip of his tongue along her lips. Then he could press her up against the cupboard, lift her leg around his hip…

She gasped, pushing at him, this time breaking the contact. She looked stunned, dazed; he felt as if someone had plied a cast iron skillet to the side of his head. He would have thought himself a complete idiot if he had any capacity for thought left.

"Sorry," he rasped out, then realized he hadn't actually done anything requiring an apology. He'd only thought it. Better to cover his bases anyway.

"No problem," she murmured, echoing his response to her earlier. She stood frozen by the breakfast bar, as if she didn't know what to do next.

He understood her confusion, since he hadn't a clue what he was supposed to be doing. Then he saw the ground beef and cans on the kitchen counter. Dinner. Right. They were about to make dinner.

Striding to the sink, he cupped water in his hands and buried his face in it. It didn't exactly return the brains to his head, but it gave him something to do that wasn't holding Lori, touching Lori. This time, he grabbed the paper towel himself, water dripping into his T-shirt. Eyes closed, he whacked his hand on the cabinet before he found the towel, but the sting brought a little more clarity into his mind.

Once he'd swiped away the water, he retrieved the onion from the sink. He held it out to Lori, still standing at the end of the breakfast bar. "Would you chop the onion? I have to get the ground beef cooking."

She just stared at him, then her gaze dropped to the pale brown globe in his hand. "Chop the onion."

"Are you still feeling dizzy?"

She shook her head. "I'm fine."

He set the onion on the counter. Better not to risk another touch. "The cutting boards are down there." He pointed to a cabinet under the sink.

She bent carefully, pulled out a wooden cutting board and set it on the counter. She positioned the onion in the center of the board. "I guess I need a knife."

He tugged open the knife drawer, indicated the large chef's knife. She plucked it from the tray, then held it out as if she'd never used one before.

She took hold of the onion, held the knife aloft. Turned the onion over. Gave it another one-eighty. Rested the knife blade against the papery skin. Then finally, set the knife down carefully beside the onion.

"I feel like a total idiot." She picked up the onion, gestured at him with it. "I have no idea how to chop this."

Chapter Seven

Gabe's brow furrowed. "I'm not fussy. Cut it any way you like."

Why did he have to be so obtuse? Frustrated and embarrassed, Lori held the onion out to him. "I don't know how at all. I've never done it."

"Never chopped an onion."

She shook her head, feeling like a fool. Rattled already by her dizzy spell, then the sizzling tension between them when he'd come to her aid, she felt as scrambled as a margarita in a blender.

He reached for the tomato and cucumber. "You can make the salad. Cut these up."

She let him plop them into her hands. She wanted to throw them back at him. "I don't know how to cook. At all."

He didn't believe her, she could see it in his face. "How could a thirty-year-old woman—"

"Thirty-two."

"—get through life without learning to cook?"

She didn't want to have this conversation. Her stomach churned, on the edge of nausea, and she used that as an excuse to stall. Tugging open the pantry cupboard door, she found the soda crackers and took her time opening the package.

"I never had a chance to learn." She bit into the cracker. "Not while I was growing up. And when I was drinking…"

"More of a liquid diet." He said the words dryly. She caught the trace of a smile.

"When I wasn't living at home, I had takeout. Ate at restaurants."

"Expensive, for someone living on their own."

"I had a generous allowance."

His faint smile vanished. "You found someone to support you." There was an edge to his tone. "I'm sure it was a fair exchange."

She met his cold gaze with one of her own. "My parents. Not a man."

He leaned back against the kitchen counter. She set aside the veggies he'd handed her and pulled around one of the bar stools on the other side of the breakfast bar. She positioned it at the opposite end of the counter from him.

"You've heard of HNN?"

"Yeah. They own several cable channels. I watch their sports channel once in a while."

"Hightower National Network is a television and radio conglomerate. Richard Hightower is my father."

"So you're rolling in it."

"Not me. My parents."

He acknowledged the distinction with a nod. With most men, when they learned who she was, the dollar signs would flash in their eyes. Gabe seemed completely unimpressed by the Hightower millions.

He crouched to open the cabinet under the counter. "Your parents have a problem with you learning to cook?"

"We had a full-time chef. I just never got the chance."

Straightening again, he set a skillet on the stove. "What did they expect you to do when you moved out on your own?"

"They didn't expect me to move out. At least not until I married."

The capable motions of his hands fascinated her as he crumbled the ground beef into the skillet. "And did you?"

Her stomach clenched. "Yeah."

"Didn't they expect you to cook for your husband?"

She laughed, a bitter sound. "They expected me to choose the right husband so I wouldn't have to."

Once all the meat was in the skillet and the burner turned on, Gabe washed up at the sink. Then he slid the cutting board with the onion still on it over toward her.

"Here's your first cooking lesson, then." He held out the knife handle to her. She took it, the tool feeling foreign in her hand. "Cut it in half first, lengthwise." He pointed to indicate what he meant. "Cut out the core. That'll make it easier to peel."

It was such a simple task, but learning how to chop an onion seemed like a revelation to Lori. Her parents' protection of her for her entire life robbed her of an essential tool—competency. Confidence in her own ability.

The pieces of onion she slid back across the counter toward Gabe were uneven in size, but she'd done it herself. She even had the tears flowing from her eyes to prove it.

Setting down the knife, Lori moved to rub the moisture from her eyes with her fingers. Gabe grabbed her wrist. "Don't. You have to wash your hands first."

He tore a paper towel from the roll and dabbed gently at her eyes. His fingers still circled her wrist, warming her.

He set aside the wad of paper, but he didn't let her go. He leaned closer across the counter, his thumb stroking her cheek. She felt the moisture trail as he swiped away a tear that had spilled down her face.

He'll let go now, she thought, although she didn't want to lose the contact. But as his hand lingered against her cheek, she couldn't resist the impulse to press into it, to feel his palm cup her face. Her eyes drifted shut, his heat more drugging than alcohol and just as forbidden.

"Lori."

Her name was a ragged, tattered bit of sound, as if he could barely get the breath to speak it. Sensation curled low in her body, and she was both grateful for the barrier between them and frustrated by it.

She wrapped her fingers around his wrist, intending to pull his hand away from her face. But the moment she felt his warm, hair-roughened skin, the play of tendons against her palm, she couldn't follow through. Instead she moved her hand up his arm, feeling the muscles shift, the changing textures as she absorbed every inch along the way from wrist to shoulder.

She kept her eyes shut, not wanting to see what was in his face. If it was discomfort, unease, she'd rather not know. If it was an answering heat, she knew it would only stoke her fire higher.

"Lori."

She couldn't resist the demand of her softly spoken name. She opened her eyes, then stared, stunned by the sharpness of his desire. An answering flame flared inside her.

The first touch of his lips on hers was so featherlight, it stole the breath from her lungs. Her fingers tightened, reflexively pulling him closer. At her implicit invitation, he deepened the kiss, slanting his mouth across hers, sucking gently. Then his tongue dove inside, wet and hot, and she knew she was lost.

She had to stop this, couldn't let it continue. But she had no control over her own body, the way her hips thrust toward him, her breasts pressed against his firm chest. She wanted all of him in that instant, was ready to abandon herself to him in return. Sensation filled her universe, crowding out thought.

He drew back, gasping, his expression shellshocked. She understood the silent query in his dazed green eyes. It was up to her to break this off. If she let him kiss her again, they wouldn't stop until they'd both reached completion.

Her will nearly gone, she dropped her hand from him, breaking the connection. He pulled away and by the time she'd worked up the courage to look at him, he'd turned to the stove, tending to the meat crackling in the skillet.

She pushed off her stool. "Excuse me." There was no way she could sidle up next to him to wash her hands at the kitchen sink. She escaped to the bathroom instead.

When she returned, the pile of chopped onions was gone, replaced by the tomato and cucumber. He stayed by the stove as he talked her through the task of preparing veggies for a salad. When he handed her a bowl, he kept his distance, then washed and cored the head of lettuce himself without comment.

The salad tossed in the bowl, Lori watched Gabe put together the sauce, combining the meat and onions with the cans of tomatoes in a large pot. He measured herbs into his palm, then tossed those in, their fragrance filling the kitchen. Giving the sauce a final stir, he turned down the burner and set a lid on the pot.

He rinsed the wooden spoon, then set it on the stove. "Should probably give that a half hour or so."

"Is there anything else I can do?"

The look he gave her sent a shiver up her spine. "The spaghetti's in the pantry. Second shelf."

As she looked through the cupboard for the pasta, she could feel his gaze on her. But when she turned with the box of spaghetti, he was at the sink, filling a pot with water.

She handed over the box. "I thought I'd go sit on the back deck. If you don't need anything else?"

You, Gabe thought. *I need you.*

He turned away from her and set the box beside the stove. "There's nothing else."

Except the feel of your skin. The sound of your breathing and how it changes when I touch you.

The urgency to take her hand, to pull her into him raged inside him. He could still feel her against his palm, the stroke of her fingers up his arm.

He lifted the lid on the pot of water, then dropped it with a clatter when the metal handle burned his hand. Fumbling in the drawer for a pot holder, he tried again. The water wasn't quite boiling yet. "I'll let you know when it's ready."

She slipped out the back door and his body's clamoring for her finally eased. It didn't disappear completely, wouldn't until she'd headed back to her life and he to his. But that was still at least a week away. Meanwhile, not even cold showers could save him from her fire.

It didn't help that he'd been stupid enough to touch her when she'd been about to rub her eyes. He could justify that contact; her hands were covered with the onion's essence and he didn't want her to compound her discomfort. But then to wipe away her tears, to curve his hand around her face…what kind of idiot was he to subject himself to that kind of torture?

She kept surprising him. That she came from money was a no-brainer; he'd guessed as much. That she seemed to want to distance herself from it, that she wanted to count every penny and pay her own way didn't fit the rich girl upbringing. Tyrell's wife, Sadie, didn't either, but Sadie's folks had insisted she work for the extras she wanted in life rather than pay her way. It seemed Lori's parents had smoothed the way for her every step, and Lori never had to lift a finger.

He didn't want to like her. It would just complicate things, make his attraction for her that much more difficult to ignore. But admiration for her had taken hold—for her strength, her determination to make her own life her own way.

Still, what did he really know about her? For all he knew, she and her parents were having a spat and they'd temporarily cut her off from her trust fund. She was having a taste of life on her own and putting on a good act to garner his sympathy. The notion was cynical as hell, but it wasn't as if he hadn't been fooled by a woman before.

Krista had seemed so sweet, so giving when he'd first met her, his first year out of the academy. Fresh-faced and pretty in a girl-next-door kind of way, she'd made him feel on top of the world when they were first dating. Their six-week courtship had led to a hasty marriage when she'd gotten pregnant. But they'd both been thrilled at the prospect of a child— or so he'd thought.

He'd been the first to hold Brandon. The squalling, red-faced baby boy, six pounds, fifteen ounces of indignant humanity, had Gabe's heart in his tiny fist from day one.

He blanked his mind before it ventured into dangerous territory—imagining what Brandon might look like now. That would only break his heart.

Instead he uncovered the pot of now boiling water and dumped the box of spaghetti into it. Poking the stiff strands down under the surface with the wooden spoon, he grasped hold of the mundane to protect him from the agony of the past. Those claws never seemed to quite let go.

As the pasta simmered, he let his mind drift back to Lori, the lesser of two evils. He wondered what was really going on with her—the dizziness, the nausea, the too-pale complexion. Maybe it had been more than alcohol on her back and she was still experiencing withdrawal.

She didn't have that jitteriness about her he usually saw in drug addicts. She wasn't a smoker either—surprising since plenty of ex-drinkers used cigarettes as something to reach for instead of that next highball. Something swam beneath the surface of that near-perfect face, something that tempted him to dive deeper.

But he wouldn't. He had enough on his own plate to handle without taking on someone else's headaches. Testing a strand of pasta, he grabbed the colander from the cupboard and set it in the sink. The contents of the pot dumped into the colander, he headed for the back door to tell Lori dinner was about ready.

She'd fallen asleep on the chaise lounge, her face tipped down, her hands slack at her sides. The book she'd been writing in earlier had fallen open and a twinge of curiosity urged him to read a page.

He shut the book without registering so much as a word. Ten years ago, he'd spilled his own thoughts out into a journal, as directed by the therapist he'd finally let Tyrell talk him into seeing. The words he scrawled were so hateful, so violent, they horrified him and despite the therapist's urging to let his pain spill onto the page instead of holding it inside, he burned the book a few weeks into therapy.

A lock of Lori's silky blond hair had slipped across her face and before he could even think, he'd gone down on one knee and reached out to sweep the silvery-gold strands back into place. He gave in to the temptation to touch her, but only long enough to tuck the satiny lock away from her eyes and back behind her ear.

She stirred, then opened her eyes. He had his hand back at his side by then, but damned if he didn't feel guilty.

"Dinner's ready." He stepped back and away from her, heading for the open back door.

"Gabe." He looked back; she had the journal in her hand. "Did you—"

"No. I didn't."

"Good," she said softly.

Tucking the journal under her arm, she rose. He waited for her, let her go in before him. He tried to tell himself it wasn't to have her close, to catch a whiff of whatever scent seemed to drift from her like an aura. He didn't buy his own rationalization.

They ate dinner at the breakfast bar, their conversation limited to "Could you pass the salad?" and "Do you want another glass of water?" She actually ate a healthy portion, the first time he'd seen her eat like a real person with a real appetite.

When she offered to do the dishes, he let her, but he didn't hang around to supervise. He was far too captivated by her graceful motions as she gathered up the plates and serving bowls then carried them to the sink. Last thing he needed was to stand there, gaping, while she worked.

Instead he went back out to the deck and collected his tools, stacking the leftover lumber along the wall of the house. The sun had settled at the tops of the pines, on its way to sunset. A mosquito whined in his ear, another one took the opportunity to chomp on his arm. If he didn't get inside, he'd be a meal for every flying annoyance in the general area.

She was just drying her hands when he pushed open the back door and stepped into the kitchen. He should just keep going, head for his bedroom and hibernate in there the rest of the evening. He hadn't wired that television to the satellite system yet, but he'd brought a couple books he'd been meaning to read. The radio got a couple of stations; he could read and listen to jazz until bedtime.

But he got as far as the breakfast bar and couldn't seem to persuade his feet to go any farther. Her gaze met his and he could see the expectation in her eyes. He tried to figure out what to say, but his brain seemed to fixate on the slenderness of her body, the enticing angles of her face.

"I thought I'd see if there's a ballgame on tonight." The words came out without any real thought, but it seemed like such a good idea, he went with it. "Watch it on the big screen."

Her gaze wary, she rumpled the paper towel in her hands. "What kind of ballgame?"

"Baseball. Maybe the Giants." A familiar pain stabbed at him as an image hovered in his mind's eye. Brandon in the seat beside him at Dodger Stadium. A grin on his face, the two of them sharing a bag of peanuts. Except it had never happened that way.

Suddenly he couldn't bear the thought of sitting in front of that television alone. He'd go to his room, read instead. He spun away, started toward the hallway.

"I'll watch with you." Her sweet voice clutched at his heart. "Although I don't know much about baseball."

He turned to face her. "You're wearing a Giants sweatshirt. I figured you were a fan."

She looked down at it, as if surprised by the emblem emblazoned across it. "The kids at the teen center gave it to me. They pooled their money to buy it."

"Let's see if they're playing, then." He stepped into the great room and tracked down the remote.

She came out and sat on the sofa facing the large television, folding her feet under her at one end. Switching on the TV, Gabe flipped through the on-screen satellite schedule, searching for the sports channels.

"Looks like the Giants game is blacked out. How about the Padres and the Astros?"

Her throaty laugh prickled up his spine. "Since I don't know one team from another, that sounds fine."

He selected the appropriate channel and dropped the remote on the sofa. "You want something to drink?"

"Some water would be great."

Why did everything out of her mouth sound like an invitation for sex? He headed for the kitchen and grabbed a cola from the fridge, then served her up a glass of water. Setting the water on the side table next to her, he slumped into the cushions on the other end of the sofa, as far from her as possible.

She sipped at her water. "I confess I'm not entirely ignorant about baseball. They hit the ball with a bat, they run around the bases, if it goes over the fence it's a home run."

He took a swallow of soda, the carbonation burning his tongue. "Only if it's in fair territory."

"And fair territory would be…" She smiled at him.

Fair would be if she'd stop using that lethal weapon of a smile. "The wedge between first and third."

"I think I'm having a blonde moment. I haven't a clue what you mean."

"Growing up in the Bay Area, you never went to a Giants game?"

"That was a little too lowbrow for our household.

Although…" Her brow furrowed. "Hightower had local broadcast rights to the games for a few years. I have a vague memory of sitting in a luxury box at Candlestick."

"How old were you?"

"Four? Five? I just remember being miserable in the dress my mother made me wear."

He tried to imagine her at four or five. That bright blond hair, those wide brown eyes. She would have melted the heart of any grown-up.

"You don't remember the game at all?"

She shook her head, her mouth curving in a faint smile. "I think I ate too much popcorn. I threw up on someone's shoes." Her sigh seemed weighted by time and memory. "Not the first time I mortified my parents. They didn't take me to any other games."

"A lot to expect of a four-year-old in a crowd of strange adults."

She shrugged. "They were used to my older sister. She pretty much behaved like a grown-up from the day she was born." She focused on the television screen. "So fair territory…"

He rose to trace the first- and third-base lines on the screen, pointing out the foul poles on either side. He explained pop flies and sacrifice flies, bunts and hitting into the gap. When she asked why a particular batter with a better than .250 average went for a squeeze play instead of hitting away, he realized she was far sharper than she gave herself credit.

She started to droop during the bottom of the eighth. With her head resting on the back of the sofa, her eyes would drift shut a moment before she forced them open again. He could almost picture that blond four-year-old, too tired to stay awake, but too excited to let herself sleep.

She finally gave up the ghost, her neck bent at an awkward angle and her chest rising and falling evenly as she slept. He'd have to wake her eventually. If she stayed that way all night she'd have a hellacious stiff neck in the morning. But she looked so peaceful, so relaxed, he waited until the Padres beat the Astros in the top of the ninth.

Shutting off the television, he slid to her end of the sofa. Watching her, he wanted to tug her into his arms, hold her against him, feel her warmth, her softness. Except in the past several months when despair over his son had pushed him deep into darkness, he hadn't exactly been a monk when it came to women. But the women he'd been with had been nothing more than acquaintances, as willing as he to engage in casual sex. He hadn't been to bed with a woman he cared about since Krista.

He shouldn't have a heart left after Krista, shouldn't be capable of feeling anymore. At least not for a woman. He had to reserve all his feelings, all his emotions for his son. But Lori…

She stirred, shifting, straightening her slender neck, finding a more comfortable position. He could leave her, let her wake on her own, get herself to bed. She wasn't his responsibility. Hadn't they established that at the outset?

He found himself reaching for her, his hand cupping her shoulder, squeezing as he gave her a gentle shake. She edged away from him, like a child reluctant to wake. "Lori," he murmured.

Her eyes opened slowly, then fixed on him, still

dark and liquid with sleep. With the television off, the small table lamp at the other end of the sofa provided the only illumination in the room. The pale yellow light edged her hair with gold, warmed her face to an irresistible cream.

Somehow, his hand had moved up to caress her cheek, his thumb tracing across her face, along her jaw-line, to the corner of her mouth. It would be a big mistake to touch her lips, that would only lead him closer to thinking about what it would be like to kiss her. But that thought burned in his mind anyway, whether or not he tested the softness of her mouth with his thumb.

He must have some restraint left, somewhere down deep where his common sense resided. But logic and common sense had taken a powder, refused to raise that wagging finger that would have stopped the craziness. Nothing was left but the sensation of his palm against her silky skin, the fire in her dark brown gaze, the sound of her breathing stroking along his nerves.

He would just brush his lips against hers again. He wouldn't take the kiss any further and give in to temptation a second time, no matter how good it felt. But the moment of friction between his mouth and hers crashed into him with the force of a grand-slam home run, and pulling away seemed impossible. He had to taste her, to part her lips with his tongue, dive inside and lose himself.

She lifted her hands to his chest, and he tensed, breath held as he waited for her to push him away. When her fingers curled, clutching his shirt, the air left his lungs and his heart jetted into overdrive. The pleasure of her nearness overwhelmed him until he could feel, see, hear nothing but her.

He drew his mouth from side to side over hers, the sensation of moist satin an agonizing sweetness. Her heat threatened to incinerate him—under his hands, radiating into his chest where she touched him, in the connection point of her mouth against his. Desire cut low in his body, filling his flesh, sending him close to flashpoint.

All from what was scarcely even a kiss. The bare contact was so sweet, he wanted it to go on forever, even as his body urged him to go further, press harder, his tongue against hers, plunging inside.

The firmer pressure of her hands against his chest didn't register at first. He was too caught up in her scent, the moist softness of her mouth. But when she pushed harder, reason dropped over him like a drenched blanket and he rose and stumbled back away from her. She looked as shocked at what had happened as he felt.

"God, I'm sorry." He swiped at his face, trying unsuccessfully to wipe away the feel of her. "I shouldn't have…I'm sorry."

He edged away, then hurried down the hall to his own bedroom. Grabbing up the sweats he'd brought to sleep in, he crossed the hall to the bathroom. Another cold shower and maybe he'd get his head on straight.

But the iciest water wouldn't drown the emotions he'd been stupid enough to let loose. That was a fire far more dangerous and much more difficult to put out.

Chapter Eight

She'd told herself two lies. The first had really been more wishful thinking than out-and-out untruth. She'd really thought her nausea had finally faded, that if she was nice to her stomach and fed it regular meals, it would be nice in return. Crouched over the toilet now, the second morning after the night of infamy when she'd watched the ballgame with Gabe, she acknowledged that all her wishing hadn't made it a reality.

The second lie was the more blatant one—that it had meant nothing when Gabe had brushed his lips against hers, that it had been inadvertent, happenstance, unintended. He'd been leaning over, trying to wake her, he'd slipped. His mouth had fallen against hers accidentally. It hadn't lingered there, his breath mingling with hers, his heat soaking into her.

Of course, it had been more than an accidental brush of his mouth. It had been a prelude, a precursor to pleasure. In another moment, that scudding touch would have led to a sensual assault from which it would have been impossible to break free. She'd been close to lost with the first contact.

It had felt about as good as this session in the bathroom felt bad. It had taken every ounce of willpower in her to push him away, when all she wanted was to pull him even closer. She might fool herself into thinking it hadn't been a real, actual kiss, but it had had her tossing and turning for the two nights since.

She shifted, leaning her back against the vanity cabinet, waiting to see if her stomach had finished its argument or if it was prepping for round two. There were still a few crackers left in the nightstand drawer, although they hadn't done the trick this morning.

Maybe she'd try getting to her feet. Reaching for the edge of the vanity for support, a rap on the bathroom door startled her and she whacked her elbow against the cabinet.

"What's going on in there?" Gabe's voice through the shut door rippled along her nerve endings.

Outrage followed on the heels of her reaction to him. "Why are you in my bedroom?"

"You came out, you ran back in. You left the door open."

So she had. Her nausea hadn't hit until she'd gotten a whiff of whatever Gabe had been cooking for his breakfast.

The memory sent a twist of queasiness through her. She dropped her head in her hand and dragged in a breath. "Go away."

He opened the door, glancing in carefully as if afraid he'd catch her undressed. She was, in a way, completely stripped of her dignity as she slumped on the floor.

His face hardened as he stared down at her. "You're sick to your stomach."

She forced herself to look up at him. "Guilty as charged."

His eyes were like ice. "I heard you get up last night."

"I was thirsty. I got a glass of water."

"You opened the liquor cabinet."

For a moment, shock struck her silent. Then indignation exploded inside her and every angry denial she'd ever concocted over the years flooded her brain. In the end, she took a breath, counted to ten.

"I wasn't drinking." She kept her tone even, drained it of the self-righteousness that wanted to creep in. "Not anything but water, anyway. It was just easier to grab a glass from the wet bar."

He stared at her, and she could see him weigh her words, searching for the truth. She wondered why he seemed to care so much. She wondered why *she* did.

"Then why are you sick?"

Why not tell him? Lay out for him how her naive stupidity got her into a mess she now had to resolve. Garner his sympathy, put on the sad face she'd so often used to manipulate her parents, her sister, her friends so they would race to her aid.

Her stomach, empty and aching, lurched at the thought. As much as she'd come to hate evasions of the truth, the sidestepping that smacked too closely of the daily dance she'd done with her parents to avoid telling them about the latest bonehead mistakes she'd made, she hated her dependency even more.

Tired of wallowing in misery on the floor, she levered herself up, rising slowly. She was relieved when she got to her feet that her stomach had decided to behave.

She washed her face and swished water in her mouth before turning back to him. "I'm a little anemic, that's all." That much was true.

His gaze cut straight through her. "That doesn't explain the nausea."

"A bug. I'm still getting over it." That was a further stretch. What she suffered from wouldn't clear up for at least another seven months.

"You ought to see a doctor."

"I am. She's on top of it." She edged past him, slipping from the bathroom.

Gabe followed her through the bedroom and into the great room. "You're passing out. Throwing up. Does she know?"

In the kitchen, she opened the refrigerator and took out the milk. It was nearly empty. She couldn't even take care of herself enough to keep milk in the fridge.

Gabe's inquisition coupled with her feelings of ineptitude sent irritation rushing through her. "Why is this any of your business?"

His gaze narrowed on her. "Because if you're going to swoon at my feet, I'd like to know why." He pulled a glass from the cupboard and handed it to her.

The milk barely wet the bottom of the glass. She fought back the ridiculous urge to cry. "It's not serious. I'm handling it." She drank the milk in one swallow then rinsed the glass.

"That's a matter of opinion."

"It's not your job to worry about me." Tugging open the fridge again, she retrieved the orange juice. What was left nearly filled the glass. She sipped at the tart liquid, praying her stomach wouldn't rebel.

"I just want you to be straight with me, Lori."

"What does it matter to you?"

"I don't know. It shouldn't." He flicked a glance out the kitchen window. "But it does."

Setting aside the glass of juice, she leaned against the counter, hugging herself. "Have you ever trusted someone, and it went all wrong?"

She might as well have slapped him, he looked so thunderstruck. A silent beat later, he answered, "Yes."

"You really thought you loved them, thought you could believe in them, then they cut you so deep—"

"I can't do this." His eyes were wild, his jaw stiff with tension. "Can't do this."

He strode from the kitchen then and out to the back deck, the noise of the slamming door punctuating the quiet.

She'd blindsided him, that was all.

She hadn't known what her idle question would do, how it would wrench the past up and slam it in his face. Surprise was the only reason it hurt as much as it did, surprise and the most recent roadblock he'd come up to Tahoe to confront. If he hadn't already been so vulnerable, Lori's simple question would never have broken open the box he'd so neatly built around his pain the past ten years.

Numbness. That was his escape from the pain. He would build it back around his heart, construct the barriers again. He wouldn't think about Lori's question about trust, wouldn't think of Krista's betrayal, his mad rush through an empty house. He wouldn't think of his son.

Gabe paced the length of the deck, restless energy pulling him in a hundred directions. He ought to go back inside to finish his breakfast. He'd only had a couple bites of the eggs he'd scrambled before he went looking for Lori in the bathroom. The rest of them were probably stone-cold along with the toast he'd made and the coffee he'd poured. His appetite gone, he'd probably end up dumping the lot into the trash.

The last day and a half, everything had seemed wrong. He never should have kissed Lori; he'd known it then and it had only been driven home in the intervening hours. He'd barely slept the past two nights and as a consequence he'd been a real hazard with the circular saw. Yesterday he'd had to switch gears, putting aside the deck repairs to focus on the less risky task of running the cable to hook up the television in the back bedroom.

Which meant he could watch the ballgames or whatever crummy old movie came on at 2:00 a.m. in his own room, safe from the temptation of Lori. It didn't help him sleep, but at least his mind was occupied by the boob tube instead of the blonde sleeping in the master bedroom.

Today didn't look like a good day for power tools either. Out back, there was a pile of oak from a tree downed by last winter's storm. Tyrell had gotten it cut up one recent weekend when he and Sadie were visiting the chalet, now it only needed stacking. That seemed like a safe enough task to occupy him this morning.

But first, he had to clean up from breakfast, which meant facing Lori again. He stepped inside, half hoping she'd have finished in the kitchen and holed up in her room again. But she was seated at the breakfast bar, spreading peanut butter on a slice of toast. She froze when she saw him, then her hand slipped and she smeared peanut butter on her finger. Setting aside the knife, she sucked her finger clean.

Desire pounded inside him. "Don't do that."

"What?" She looked down at her hand, then color rose in her cheeks. "Sorry." She wiped at her fingers with her paper napkin.

"No." He rubbed a hand over his face. "Not your fault. I just..." He was just too damn horny. "Listen...the other night..."

The pale pink in her cheeks deepened. "Yes?"

"I'm sorry. I don't know why..." Of course he knew why. She drove him crazy with need. She was too female, too beautiful, too perfect. None of it her fault. "Look, it's not my way to...take advantage."

"You didn't. Not really. A couple of kisses—hardly anything."

They would have been something pretty damn quick. "I shouldn't be touching you."

"You won't. Anymore."

"I won't." He wasn't exactly sure how he would keep that promise, but maybe he'd take a page from the twelve-step book—one day at a time.

She kept her wary gaze on him another moment, then bent her head to her breakfast. He stared, mesmerized, as she took a bite then licked a bit of peanut butter from her mouth. He tore his gaze away, grabbing up his plate.

About to dump the contents in the garbage, he slid the plate in the microwave instead. After a few seconds nuking, he slapped the eggs inside the two slices of toast. He wasn't the least bit hungry, but he had to have fuel for the day's work. It was bad enough he hadn't had enough sleep last night. He didn't have to compound it by working on an empty stomach.

Wrapping a paper towel around the makeshift sandwich, he started for the door. "I'll be out back stacking wood." He made sure he didn't look at her again.

As he crossed the deck and headed down the stairs, he forced down a bite of his sandwich. As unappetizing as the cardboard toast and rubbery eggs were, eating gave him something to think about besides the tip of Lori's tongue licking a smudge of peanut butter from her mouth. It was almost enough of a distraction to stop himself thinking of how those soft lips would feel against his own tongue.

Lori had finished her breakfast, cleaned up the few dishes she'd used, written up a list for the market, read two chapters in one of the books she'd picked up at the used book store and left a message for Amy to call her back at lunchtime. She couldn't think of anything else to keep her inside and frankly, she was going stir-crazy with her enforced solitude.

She yearned to go outside, soak up the sun on the deck, maybe hike back down to the lake and enjoy the cool peace beside Tahoe's crystalline blue water. But going outside meant facing Gabe again. The powerful jolt of her maddening awareness of him made even the jitteriness of being trapped inside seem soothing by comparison.

Slipping into the master bedroom, she peered through the slider overlooking the deck to look for him. She spied the hodgepodge pile of oak just beyond the overhang of the deck, two gloved hands appearing and disappearing as Gabe picked up pieces to relocate them. Considering the size of the pile still remaining, he'd be at his task for another hour or so. If she set up the chaise on the other side of the house, she'd have the privacy there she needed. If she could get some of her thoughts down on paper, maybe they'd stop whirling and tumbling in her mind.

Her journal tucked under her arm, she stepped out onto the back deck. Folding the chaise with her journal inside it, she circled around the side of the house. Behind her, the clunk of wood tossed in a pile filtered toward her, a reminder of Gabe only a few feet away.

As she rounded the corner of the chalet, she noticed an *X* of orange paint marking a weathered bit of decking and she stepped to one side of it. The deck seemed to give way slightly under her left foot, creaking and cracking. Startled, she jumped aside, landing heavily on her right foot, the chaise jarring from her hands.

The snap of wood went through her body like a shock and as the deck swallowed up her leg, she screamed in sudden terror. The redwood seemed to crumble all around her, her weight shattering the dry-rotted lumber. As she fell to her waist through the growing hole of the deck, one thought seared itself into her brain.

My baby.

The moment he heard her scream, Gabe took off running, a piece of oak still gripped in each hand. As he pelted for the stairs, he tossed the wood aside, then took the steps three at a time. He caught a glimpse of the chaise lounge, askew beside the house, but couldn't see Lori.

Horror filled him when he rounded the corner. Lori was jammed nearly to her shoulders in a broken outhole in the deck, her splayed arms the only thing keeping her from falling farther. The wood around her still groaned from her weight.

Relief flashed in her face when she saw him, then vanished when he took a step closer. "Don't! I think it's all rotted away on this side."

"Hang on. Just hang on."

He turned and ran for the steps, racing down and clearing the last three in one leap. He made a beeline for the shed, then wrenched its doors open. Throwing aside the junk leaning against the stepladder, he wrestled the metal contraption free and ran back to where Lori dangled from the deck.

He yanked open the ladder, setting it up near her. The eight-footer was short enough to fit under the deck, but tall enough for Lori's feet to reach, despite the slope of the terrain. Scooting the ladder over and steadying it on the uneven ground, he took hold of Lori's ankle.

"Here, sweetheart, put your foot here." He eased her feet to the top step, one down from the apex of the ladder. She hissed in a breath when he touched her right calf. Her jeans were torn there. "You okay?"

Her voice was a bit muffled through the deck. "I will be when I get free."

"As quick as I can."

Once he was sure she was secure on the ladder, he hurried to the front of the house and up the front steps. Snatching up the last four ten-foot lengths of two-by-six redwood, he returned to Lori.

"I'm going to build a bridge here. Just hang on."

She mustered a shaky smile. "Not much choice."

Stepping as close to the house as he could, he laid the sticks of lumber on either side of Lori's outstretched fingertips, two to her left, two to her right. "Lift your arms, Lori."

She squeezed her eyes shut for a moment. "I'd rather not."

"You're not going anywhere with the ladder under your feet. I need these close to you to get enough leverage to pull you out."

"I can't," she whispered. "I'm so scared."

Her fear stabbed his heart. "One at a time then. Can you manage that?"

Lips pressed tight, she nodded. The fingers of her right hand turning into claws, as if she could dig them deeper into the wood, she raised her left arm. He slid the two two-by-sixes over, side by side, their breadth giving him nearly a foot of span to walk closer to her.

She slammed her left arm down the moment the wood was in place. Tears had gathered in her eyes, spilled down her cheeks. She shook her head, as if impatient with the overwhelming emotion. She dug in with her left hand, determination setting her face. "Ready?" she asked.

"Ready." He shoved in the lengths of wood when she moved her arm, then straightened in anticipation of stepping closer.

Her face tipped up at him, the incipient fear in her face suddenly transformed into terror. "Gabe!" Her shoulders shifted, her arms folding upward. "The ladder!"

He heard the ladder fall with a crash and grabbed her without thinking, latching onto her wrists before she could slip farther into the hole. Rotted decking collapsed on either side of her, but the makeshift bridge across the still solid supports held their combined weight. His hands locked around her wrists and hers around his, he backed up along the supporting two-by-sixes, pulling Lori to safety.

The moment she was clear of the hole, he had his arms around her, probably holding her too tight, but he had to feel her, still warm and vital. Then he bent to lift her in his arms, carrying her around to the front of the house.

"Gabe, I can walk."

"Even your voice is shaking. I won't risk you collapsing in reaction." He shoved open the front door.

Rounding the sofa, he set her down on the cushions. She sighed heavily. "I'm supposed to take care of myself. You can't keep coming to my rescue."

"News flash. This wasn't your fault." He pulled her shoes off, then carefully peeled away her socks. "I should have done a better job checking that part of the deck."

He forced himself to focus on the task at hand—examine her, assess her injuries, decide on a course of action. That he could feel her calf muscles working beneath the denim encasing them, that he could still remember the silk of her hair brushing against his arm as he carried her, he wouldn't think about.

Tugging up the cuffs of her jeans, he exposed her legs to her knees. Her firm calves were sleeker than he'd imagined and they dipped in intriguingly at her knees. He shook off the image of drawing his finger along the bunched up denim to the V of her legs and turned his attention to her scrapes.

Her skin was raw along her left ankle bone and higher on her calf. Her right knee had taken some damage, but it was the swelling in her left ankle that had him worried.

He took her left foot gently in his hands. "You might have a sprain." Moving slowly, he flexed her ankle.

She sucked in a sharp breath. "That hurts."

"How much?"

"Scale of one to ten, ow—" She put her hands out to stop him moving it. "Seven."

Her hands warming his derailed his thoughts again. Pulling his hands away, he jump-started his brain. "You need an ice pack."

"I'll be fine."

"Once we take care of it properly you will be."

She started to rise from the sofa. "I'll get it."

Hands on her shoulders, he eased her back. "I'll take care of it." Better to get out of the room, out of reach.

In the kitchen, he filled a plastic zipper bag with water and ice. Wrapping the bag in a kitchen towel, he returned to lay it gently against her ankle. "Stay put. I have a first aid kit in my truck."

"Check the master bath. Sadie's got a huge kit under the sink."

He stepped inside her bedroom for the second time that day and a prickle of awareness fingered down his spine, just as it had earlier when he'd invaded her privacy to check on her in the bathroom. A lingering feminine fragrance teased him and he tried to close his mind to it as he had before. But he was remembering too clearly how she'd felt in his arms.

The bed seemed enormous, the no-nonsense cotton nightgown folded on the pillow impossibly sexy, the slightly rumpled covers enticing. How easy would it be to go back out to the great room, pick Lori up from the sofa, carry her in here, slip her under those inviting covers? Then lie beside her, pull her close, tug off her jeans, her T-shirt, whatever scrap of satin she wore underneath…

He scrubbed at his face. *Don't think. Don't think.* Into the bathroom, open the vanity cabinet, pull out the big white plastic box. Check the drawers for anything useful, ignore the mysterious female odds and ends Lori had tucked inside them. Back out again, through the bedroom, close off the senses, close off the imagination, close off every wild and wayward thought.

He had it nailed right up to when his hand was on the bedroom door, ready to close it behind him. He hadn't let the least X-rated thought escape, had kept his gaze fixed on his toes, had taken the shallowest of breaths to avoid taking in her scent.

But then he made a fatal mistake. Like Lot's wife, he looked back. Saw the bed. Saw Lori there, waiting for him, her perfect body curled deliciously under the covers.

Slamming the door shut, he stepped into the great room with the first aid kit covering the straining zipper of his jeans, the white plastic box the only thing hiding his folly.

Chapter Nine

Lori wanted to take the bag of ice from her swollen ankle and dump the contents on her head in an effort to cool her crazy thoughts. The moment Gabe's hands were on her, she couldn't seem to control the fantasies that followed—him stroking her legs, drawing his fingers along her thighs, higher to where she felt so sensitized. The pain of her sprained ankle should have been a deterrent to her randy thoughts, but she probably would have had to have a broken leg to ignore how Gabe made her feel.

Once the immediate terror of falling through the deck had faded, her awareness of everything around her seemed intensified as an aftereffect. Gabe's arms lifting her, holding her, the heaving of his chest as he carried her, the taut muscle flexing against her cheek. Even the sound of his breathing stroked along her nerve endings until she felt so heated she wondered if she'd burst into flame.

Maybe it had something to do with her pregnancy, with hormones or body changes. She tried to remember what it had been like the first time with her ex-husband Tom, but so much of those months were a blur. She'd laid off the drink, had faced her pregnancy with Jessie stone-cold sober, but she'd been so messed up in her mind during her marriage, sometimes she barely noticed her husband.

It hadn't been Tom's fault. He'd been a good man in a bad situation—saddled with a wife who didn't love him, who had only married him to escape a life that should have been a fairy tale. Wealthy parents, all the money she could spend, every desire satisfied. But it still seemed so wrong. She'd always felt she didn't belong in her über-perfect family.

Gabe stepped into the great room, closing her bedroom door behind him. When she'd sent him into her bathroom, she hadn't even considered what she might have left out for him to see. She'd put her toiletries away in one of the drawers; surely he wouldn't have had to look inside them. Had she set her nightgown under the pillow as she usually did? She couldn't remember.

He wouldn't quite look at her as he knelt beside the sofa and set aside the first aid kit. His cheeks were flushed as if he was embarrassed. She *had* left her nightie out. She wanted to jump from the sofa and whip the offending garment out of sight.

He removed the bag of ice and set it aside. "I found an ankle support in the drawer. Let's see if it fits."

He'd gone through the drawers, too. Seen her toothbrush, her hair gel, her prenatal vitamins. Somehow his viewing her personal items seemed terribly intimate.

Opening the Velcro on the black neoprene support, he reached for her ankle. She edged her foot aside and took the support from his hands. "I'll do it."

She couldn't have him touch her again. Setting her

foot inside the neoprene brace, she snugged the Velcro straps around her instep and ankle.

"Better?" he asked, his voice a low rumble in her ear.

"Yes, thanks."

He opened the white plastic box and inventoried the contents. "Antiseptic wipes, antibiotic ointment, bandages…everything we need."

He took out a foil-wrapped wipe and tore off the top. For a brief moment of insanity, she imagined he was opening a condom. Her cheeks flamed in response.

His wrist immediately went to her forehead. "Are you feverish?"

She tipped her head away from him. "No. I'm fine." Plucking the foil packet from his fingers, she stretched out her left leg. "I can do this."

As lightly as she could, she dabbed at the scrapes on her ankle, calf and knee. Like a nurse handing implements to a surgeon, Gabe was ready with the antibiotic ointment, then the bandages. She managed to get through the process of doctoring herself without him touching her.

Then she twisted to ease herself up from the sofa and felt a sharp pain in her middle back. She gasped and settled back down.

"I think I hurt my back." Carefully pulling her T-shirt from her jeans, she had to stop when the knit clung to her wound. "I was so preoccupied with my ankle and the other scrapes, I didn't even feel it."

"Turn over. You can't reach."

Gingerly, she leaned on her elbows, resting her forehead against the sofa arm. Gabe worked as gently as possible, but she couldn't help but wince as he pulled her shirt free of her back.

"Sorry, sweetheart. Doing the best I can."

Sweetheart. He'd called her that out on the deck. She knew it meant nothing, had only used the endearment in an attempt to keep her calm, but hearing it again, something warm and soft spread inside her.

Sweetheart. Had anyone ever called her that? Not her parents, certainly; that wouldn't have been quite proper in her household. It was Lori, or Lori Anne if she'd been especially bad. Sadie's father had a whole host of sweet, funny names for his well-loved daughter—*punkin* and *honey* and *sugar.* Sadie's uncle called her *snicklefritz,* which always sent both girls into hysterics.

Finally unstuck from her scrape, Gabe raised her T-shirt to her bra strap. She sensed his hesitation. "Lori, I think I have to pull this up higher. Above your bra."

"Sure." She could barely squeeze out the word. "Go ahead."

He bunched the shirt just below her shoulders, then hesitated again. "I, ah, I'm going to have to…or you should…" He cleared his throat. "Your bra strap is in the way."

"Oh." The syllable was a breath of sound. "I can reach around." She tried to snake her arm back, then felt his fingers stop her.

"Don't. That'll hurt. I'll do it."

She felt the hooks give way, then he peeled away the back of the bra. Her breasts, heavy and hot, slid free of the cups. Her nipples brushed against the loose fabric.

At first she could only feel the pain of his touch as he swiped the antiseptic across her back. But he was so gentle, so tender, she forgot the soreness and felt only the stroke of his fingertips. As he ministered to her, she had to bite her lip to keep from moaning. He'd only think he'd hurt her and the last thing she wanted was for him to guess the truth.

Finally, he was finished and returning the tube of ointment to the first aid kit. "I could tape you up back here, but it would be tricky keeping it on. I think you're just as well pulling the T-shirt back over it."

"What about my bra?" Heat rose in her face as she asked the question.

"Probably ought to leave it off." The husky edge to his voice sent a tingle up her spine. "It would just rub."

"Okay." Waiting until he'd pulled the T-shirt back down again, she levered herself up. Turning slightly away, she tugged the elastic shoulder straps from under the T-shirt sleeves and off her arms. She balled the bra up in her hand.

Now her nipples grazed the knit of her T-shirt, sending sparks of sensation arrowing through her. He stared at her in utter fascination, banishing any hope that he wouldn't see her response to him.

She should get up, should leave the room. But his gaze on her was palpable as a touch, drawing her closer. Without even realizing she'd moved, she had her hand curved around the back of his neck, tugging him closer.

When his mouth settled on hers, she moaned low in her throat, the pain of her injuries fading to insignificance. If their kiss in the kitchen had burned and the one on the couch had seared, this one exploded, jolted along her nerve endings, almost unbearable in intensity. His tongue slid alongside hers, tasting, drinking, absorbing her very being.

Then his hand closed over her breast and the world rocketed out of control. Even through the T-shirt, she felt his heat, his palm grazing her nipple until it hardened into a tight bud. It felt impossibly good, and just as impossible to stop.

Digging deep, she mustered the strength to pull back, to take a breath, to ignore the taste of him still in her mouth. Pushing to her feet, she half stumbled toward the master bedroom.

"Lori."

Her name beckoned her back to the paradise of his arms, but she stayed in the bedroom doorway. "I think I'll just read in here a while." She glanced over at him.

He wouldn't look at her. "I'll get back to work then. If you're okay."

She nodded, feeling like a marionette. As she waited for him to leave, his gaze dropped to her mouth and lingered there. Her heart kicked into overdrive as she imagined him stepping inside the bedroom, pulling her into his arms, taking her to the bed.

She shut the door and leaned back against it, then jumped away when pain stabbed her back. She felt too restless to sit, but her sore ankle was screaming at her to rest it. She sat on the bed, putting her feet up and grabbing one of the baby books. But as she opened it to the next chapter, her brain was racing so fast she knew she'd never be able to read a word.

Grabbing the remote, she flipped on the television, hoping for some distraction there. But as she surfed through the channels, she came across a baseball game and the memory of Gabe's kiss came crowding back.

She turned off the television again and tossed the remote aside, even more agitated. Her ankle hurt, the scrapes on her back and legs burned and itched and her hands prickled with nervous energy.

Taking a breath, she settled her hands over her belly, covering her still-flat abdomen. The little nubbin inside her might be wreaking havoc with her stomach and driving her hormones into a frenzy, but somehow, she felt comforted knowing that life was growing there. No matter how wrong the circumstances of its conception, the new life inside her was a blessing and a miracle.

This was why she was here—not to pant after Gabe Walker or to contrive ways to be with him rather than find contentment in her own skin. She had this baby to think of, a decision to make. She'd never find the elusive peace within her to make the right choice if she let herself be distracted by Gabe.

She ought to call her doctor. She hadn't so much as brushed her belly when she'd fallen, but she'd been so afraid, who knew what her fear might have churned up for the baby. Better to be safe and check.

She'd left her cell phone on the breakfast bar with her purse, which meant she risked seeing Gabe again when she went after it. Digging through the clothes she'd brought, she found a loose tank top and put it on under the T-shirt. That would camouflage any embarrassing responses.

She'd just stepped from the bedroom when the front door opened. Gabe entered, her journal in his hand.

"I found it under the deck." He held it out to her.

"Thanks." She took it, holding it in front of her chest as an additional barrier. "I'd forgotten all about it."

He strode to the kitchen and filled a glass at the sink, drinking it down. "I'm going over the deck again." He set the tumbler carefully into the sink. "Check all the supports, all the fill pieces. Make sure everything is solid."

"Great." She moved to the breakfast bar to retrieve her phone.

He stared out the kitchen window. "I'm sorry I put you at risk."

"You'd marked that side. I shouldn't have gone over there."

"You wouldn't have if I'd told you it wasn't safe."

"You didn't know."

"I should have." His hands gripped the edge of the sink, the tendons in his arms taut. "I'm supposed to know what's safe. What isn't. What to trust."

"I'm fine, Gabe."

"Yeah." He nodded. "Thank God for that."

Her phone bleated in her hand and she nearly dropped it in reaction. A glance at the display told her it was Amy. She quickly pressed the connect button. "Hey. Can I call you right back?" She double-checked that Amy was in her office, then set the phone beside her purse.

Gabe was nearly out the back door. "Gabe…"

He stopped, but didn't look at her. "Yeah?"

She wanted to tell him again that she was okay, that it wasn't his fault she'd fallen. But she sensed that whatever was bothering him went far beyond what had happened in the past hour. "Thanks for doctoring me."

"You're welcome." He continued out the door. She could call him back again, but didn't know what else she'd say.

Dialing Amy's number, she headed back toward the bedroom. All during her conversation with her sponsor and later with her doctor's office, she couldn't keep Gabe's face out of her mind.

Gabe had the last of the rotted wood cut away by late afternoon, and the south side of the deck had more holes than Swiss cheese when he was finished. The pieces he'd laid across the supports to pull Lori free had been his safety net as he'd worked, meticulously checking every length of board twice to be sure he hadn't missed any.

Surveying the torn-up swath of deck, he still felt he deserved a big kick in the butt for missing the problem areas in the first place. Lori might not see his dereliction as his fault, but he knew better. It had always been his weakness—to be so focused on one thing he didn't see the danger signs somewhere else.

Like with Krista. When he'd first met her, she'd seemed so normal, sweet-natured and levelheaded. When she'd found out she was pregnant, he'd taken her giddiness as simple happiness over the baby and a sign of how much she loved him. Although the news had unsettled him at first, her joy had infected him pretty quickly and he'd been glad to marry her.

After Brandon was born, Gabe thought Krista's possessiveness with the new baby was par for the course for a first-time mother. That her jealousy extended to Gabe when Brandon grew older and wanted more time with his daddy, Gabe never realized…until after, when it was too late.

This time his focus had been on Lori, instead of the job he had come up here to do. Back when he'd met Krista, he'd been young and naive; maybe he could excuse his lack of awareness. But now he was a grown-up, not an out-of-control teenager who couldn't rein in his X-rated thoughts. And with someone's safety again at stake—Lori's—he had to keep his mind on his work. He had no business contemplating how soft her skin felt, how lush her breasts were freed from her bra.

Backing away from the damaged area, he headed down the stairs and under the deck. He'd checked underneath when he'd first started the repairs, but considering the lousy job he'd done so far, he'd better look again. Setting up the ladder, he took his time scrutinizing every support under the worst part of the damaged deck. Using a screwdriver to check for soft spots, he confirmed he hadn't missed any bad boards.

Maybe he ought to do a visual inspection of the rest of the deck, top and bottom. He'd want to pay particular notice of where he'd already made repairs. He had to make sure the dry rot wasn't more extensive than he'd thought.

He heard the front door shut and quickly descended the ladder. "Stay away from this side!" he called out as he trotted around to the front of the chalet.

She was halfway down the steps. She'd untucked her T-shirt and it billowed around her. He would have thought the concealing clothing would make her less tempting, but he only wanted to slip his hands under that baggy shirt to feel the softness beneath.

She took the last few steps. "You never came in for lunch."

"Too busy working." His stomach rumbled at the reminder. "How's the ankle?"

"Feeling better."

"You should stay off of it. Keep it elevated."

"I have been." She shifted her feet, looking off into the trees a moment before returning her gaze to him. "I'm kind of in a bind. I need a favor."

A part of him wanted to shout yes before he even knew what she wanted. "What?"

She smiled and his empty stomach did cartwheels. "Is there any way I could borrow your truck tomorrow?"

Lori hated having to ask, hated being in a position where she didn't have her own transportation. "I have an appointment in Carson City. Eleven-fifteen."

"An appointment." His gaze narrowed on her. "Another meeting?"

If she just told him yes, the discussion would be over. But she'd given up lying the day she stopped drinking. "A doctor's appointment."

"To check the ankle?"

She could say yes to that. She'd originally decided to call the doctor because of the fall. "Partly."

He stared at her, as if he could read her mind and knew she was hiding something. "I'll take you."

That was the last thing she wanted. "I've already interrupted your work too much."

"I'm going to need more lumber anyway. I'll get a better deal down in Carson."

How could she refuse? She had to get to Carson City; his truck was the only way she'd get there.

She gave in to the inevitable. "You'll let me pay for the gas then."

"It's not necessary."

"Maybe not. But I want to anyway."

She couldn't tell from his ambiguous shrug if he was accepting or refusing her offer. "Where's the doctor's office?"

"Near Carson-Tahoe Hospital. I have to be there fifteen minutes early to fill out paperwork."

"Then we should leave at ten. I can probably get a little work done before that."

"Great. Ten o'clock."

She headed back up the stairs, feeling his gaze on her until she entered the house. It wasn't until she'd settled back in her room, a baby book in her lap, that it hit her. An hour to Carson City, an hour back. All that time in the cab of Gabe's truck, with him close enough to touch.

She'd be stark raving mad by the end of the day.

The next morning, Lori thought she'd dodged the nausea bullet when the toast and tea she'd eaten for breakfast went down without difficulty. Her devious stomach waited until nine forty-five to give her trouble, sending her into the bathroom when she ought to be getting ready to leave for Carson City.

Gabe's rap on the closed bedroom door filtered into the bathroom. "Hey! You okay?"

She got to her feet and threw water on her face. A

glance in the mirror told her she looked ghastly—far too pale, her eyes shadowed hollows in her face. Maybe Gabe wouldn't notice. In her dreams.

The moment she swung open the bedroom door, his sharp gaze was on her. "What's wrong?"

"Nothing a little time won't fix."

She tried to slip past him, but he grabbed her wrist. His fingers circled it easily. "You're even thinner than you were four days ago."

She'd noticed that herself, had hoped it wasn't true. She should be gaining weight, not losing it. "I know."

"You throw up nearly everything you eat, barely take in enough in the first place to keep a bird alive."

She forced herself to meet his probing gaze. "I know."

"Then what's—" Realization lit in his green eyes. "You're pregnant."

Tempted to look away, she wouldn't let herself. "Yes."

"How far along?"

"Two months."

He nodded. "Why the big secret?"

"I don't know. I guess I just didn't want to get into the whys and wherefores."

"Your husband—"

"No husband." She tugged her wrist free and moved toward the kitchen.

He followed. "Boyfriend—"

"No boyfriend. At least not anymore."

He watched as she retrieved a glass from the cupboard. "Does he know?"

Dropping a few ice cubes into the glass, she filled

it at the sink. "He disappeared the moment he heard the happy news."

Gabe leaned a hip against the breakfast bar, arms across his chest. "He should still take responsibility."

She took careful sips of the water. "He wasn't the parenting type."

"He at least ought to be supporting you financially."

"I'd rather he stay gone." She drank down the last of the water, praying her stomach wouldn't rebel. "It simplifies my life. Makes the choices easier."

"Choices—"

"What to do when the baby is born. Whether to raise him myself or…" She stared out the window, not wanting to even consider that alternative yet. She was unwilling to even let it coalesce in her mind. That would only make it possible. She didn't want it to be possible.

When she returned her gaze to Gabe, the sudden pain in his eyes shocked her. "Do you know for sure it's a boy?" His words sounded strained.

"No, I haven't…" She searched his ashen face, wondering what agony could have drained the color from his cheeks. "It's too early. I just said him because…" She shrugged, not knowing what else to say.

He turned away, seemed to collect himself again before he returned his focus on her. "What about your parents?"

Dumping the ice from the glass, she set it aside. "I'm thirty-two years old. My parents have nothing to do with this."

"It's their grandchild."

Only the truth, but it dug deep, filling that little pot of guilt inside her that never seemed to empty. Especially when it came to her parents.

He speared her with his intense green gaze. "Have you told them?"

"No."

"Will you?"

"This is none of your concern." Without her meaning to, the old haughtiness, so reminiscent of her mother, had crept into her voice. She didn't like it.

She didn't owe him an explanation, but something about the bleakness she'd seen in his eyes drove her to give one. "I'll tell them. But first I have to decide. On my own."

His jaw was stiff with tension. "But could you really let him go?"

He strode from the kitchen then and out to the back deck, slamming the door behind him.

He shouldn't care.

It wasn't his child. It wasn't his decision. That right belonged to Lori and the unknown SOB sperm donor who had walked out on her. If she decided it would be best to give up her child for adoption, he had to respect that. Even if just the thought of it tore him up inside.

But how could anyone give up a child? If she held that miracle in her arms, her future bundled in that innocent weight, how could she let it go?

It had nearly killed him to have that promise wrenched from his own life. How could anyone voluntarily give it up?

She opened the door so quietly, he didn't realize

she'd come after him until she cleared her throat. "It's after ten," she said, hanging back in the doorway.

"Sorry. Give me just a sec. I'll meet you out front."

Watching her sidelong, he waited until she'd stepped back inside before he turned. He didn't know what emotion still was visible in his face, but he'd just as soon not risk her seeing it. He pulled the back door shut behind him, throwing the deadbolt, making sure it was securely locked. He heard her move across the great room, the soft tread of her sneakers at the edge of his hearing.

As he locked the front door, he blanked his mind to what Lori had just told him, unwilling to think about the baby she carried. For the hundredth time, he reminded himself her affairs were none of his business. It was ridiculous to mourn over the future of a baby that was a complete stranger to him.

But as he climbed into the truck and started the engine, he couldn't escape the simple truth that it still hurt like hell.

Chapter Ten

The thick pines of the Tahoe area gave way to the sparser landscape of the Eastern Sierras as the truck descended into the Great Basin toward Carson City. Emotions roiled inside Lori—worry about her upcoming doctor's visit, concern for whatever pain brewed inside Gabe and her ever-present awareness of him, made sharper by the heavy silence between them.

The OB in Carson was a close friend of her own physician in San Francisco and the two of them had come to some kind of agreement as to how she would pay for the visit. That she was so strapped for funds she had to rely on the kindness of her doctor was an awkward embarrassment. But better that than going to her parents for the money and getting herself entangled in obligations and dependency.

They turned off Highway 50 and started up Carson Street, car dealerships and storefronts lining the road on either side. It was only another ten minutes or so to the doctor's office, but if the silence continued for even another minute, Lori thought she'd go mad.

"Should I call you when I'm done at the doctor's?"

For a moment, she thought he wouldn't even answer her direct question. His hands tightened on the wheel and he kept his gaze forward as he slowed then stopped for a red light.

"How long will you be?" He said the words brusquely as if he resented the need to say them.

"I don't know. That's why I thought I ought to call."

The light changed and he eased the truck forward. He didn't speak again until they were abreast of the state capitol, its silver dome gleaming in the morning light. "I'll be back in an hour. If you're not done, I'll wait."

They reached Washington Street and he turned left, then right on Mountain. "It's at twelve hundred," she told him as they drove slowly down the street.

Turning into the drive alongside the doctor's office, he put the truck into Park and hurried around to her side. She didn't need his help getting out, but allowing him to seemed like the polite thing to do. The pleasure of his touch when he took her hand had nothing to do with it.

He let go of her the moment she stepped down onto the pavement, then returned to the driver's side. She smiled at him and turned to wave, but he was already looking over his shoulder to back out onto the street. Retracing his path on Mountain, he'd disappeared down the street before she'd even reached the office door.

Stepping inside, she encountered a waiting room full of women, some large with child, some as slim as her. Two or three had their husbands with them and they held hands, heads close together as they spoke in intimate tones.

An ache welled inside Lori, a longing for someone to be beside her, to share the ups and downs of her pregnancy. When she'd been pregnant with Jessie, Tom had wanted to be part of everything she experienced, from doctor visits to Lamaze classes, but she'd all but rejected his overtures. She'd been so lost within herself, she didn't know how to let him in.

But now, as she checked in with the receptionist and sat with a clipboard full of forms, she felt so alone among all these happy women. There was a contentment in the room, a quiet joy reflected in every woman's face. A confidence that what they were doing was exactly right.

The man next to her kissed his wife on the cheek, then rested a hand on her large belly. An image rose in Lori's mind—Gabe beside her, his arm around her shoulders, his hand on her belly. Him smiling at her, adoring her, adoring the baby inside her.

With a sense of panic, she shut down the fantasy. It was as if she stood at the top of an icy slope, where one wrong step would send her tumbling to the bottom. She was in this on her own, had to handle her pregnancy and what came after by herself. Imagining how different it would be with Gabe alongside her would only make the pain more difficult to bear.

Bending her head to the paperwork in her lap, she picked up the pen and started to write. For the moment, she wouldn't think of anything but the tedious task of filling out forms.

It had hit him hard when he'd pulled away from the chalet. When Lori had fallen through the deck, had injured herself due to his negligence, she could have hurt her baby as well. Until that moment when they turned onto the access road from the chalet's gravel drive, the full ramification of Lori's accident hadn't sunk in.

What if the fall had harmed her baby? As he drove with her to Carson City, the shock waves of that possibility played out in his mind. He relived the terror of what had happened over and over again—Lori falling through the deck, her pain, her fear for herself, her baby. That he hadn't actually seen her fall only made it worse. His imagination filled in the details far more vividly than his memory could.

Guilt had frozen him in his seat, glued his hands rigidly to the wheel of the truck. It ate away at him, silencing him. What could he say to her when he'd been responsible for putting her baby at risk?

When they'd reached the doctor's office, it had been all he could do to stop himself from staying with her. He was desperate to know if the fall had created a problem with her pregnancy. He'd be burning with the guilt until he knew for certain she was okay.

But he'd forced himself to leave her, had headed off to run the errands he'd used as an excuse to drive with her to Carson. The big box home improvement store at the south end of town had everything he needed, much cheaper than it would have been in Tahoe. That justified his coming with her. He could feel good about saving Tyrell a little money, even though he'd overbought the lumber, wanting to be sure he had enough in the event he discovered another mess of dry rot.

All during his shopping trip he'd checked his watch every few minutes, anxious to keep to the hour he'd told Lori. The checkout seemed interminable, loading his truck took forever. He was already late when he started back toward the doctor's office, and he had to discipline himself to drive carefully when he just wanted to race back.

She was out front when he pulled up and his heart sank when he drew close enough to see her face. She looked shaken, her eyes red as if she'd been crying. A horror filled him—the fall had been worse for her than they'd thought, she might lose the baby.

Shoving the truck into Park at the curb, he climbed out and trotted over to her. He didn't even think, just put his arms around her and held her tight. She sagged into him, the steel he sometimes saw in her gone, her vulnerability breaking his heart.

"The baby," he rasped out and his heart thundered in his chest as he waited for her response.

With Gabe's arms around her, the tight ball of pain inside her started to release. "He's fine." She forced the words past her tears. "For now. The doctor's worried."

"The fall—"

"It's not that." The OB had assured her that since there was no impact to her abdomen, the incident on the deck wasn't an issue. "The baby came through just fine."

Gabe drew back, brushing her tears away with his thumb. "Then?"

"I've lost nearly ten pounds when I should be gaining." She could still feel the shock of seeing the number on the doctor's scale. "I'm severely anemic. He said if I don't start eating right and keeping it down, it will start to affect the baby's development."

He tucked her head under his chin. A sweet warmth blossomed inside her as she drew in his scent. His embrace didn't mean anything beyond a simple gesture of comfort, but she couldn't help but yearn for more. "I don't know what to do."

She hated the desperation in her tone, the weakness. She shouldn't be leaning on him, shouldn't rely on his strength. But in that moment, it was hard enough to stand at all, let alone on her own two feet.

He eased back from her. "Let's go."

His face set with determination, he helped her into the truck, then crossed to the driver's side. As he pulled away, Lori looked over at him, saw the taut line of his jaw, the tension in his broad shoulders.

Was he angry? Did he regret holding her, resent her dumping her problems on him? "I'm sorry," she told him as he stopped at a red light.

His head whipped toward her, his gaze sharp. "For what?"

"This isn't your concern. I drag you all the way to Carson, cry on your shoulder—"

"There's nothing to apologize for."

You wouldn't know it from the stiffness of his spine, Lori thought. He gunned the truck away from the green light, then quickly changed into the right lane. She had to steady herself with a hand on her seat when he veered into the parking lot of a supermarket.

Anger seemed to brew just beneath the surface as he navigated the serpentine rows of cars in search of an empty spot. When he killed the engine, he turned to her. "I'm buying you groceries. Not one word."

She'd barely had time to recover while he rounded the back of the truck, then opened her door. "You can't spend your money on me."

"I'm not listening, Lori."

She half expected him to yank her from the cab of the truck, but he simply took her hand and held it as she stepped down. "Listen or don't," she told him as she moved aside to let him shut the door, "I pay my own way."

"Pay me back, then. But today, I'm buying you groceries."

At the entrance to the market, he grabbed a shopping cart and shoved it along in front of him. The situation had spun out of control starting with her tears in front of the doctor's office and her giving in to his touch when he took her into his arms. Somehow a man had taken charge of her life again, and she'd barely put up a token resistance.

"Gabe—"

He stopped short and she bumped into him, the rock-hard muscles of his back reminding her how angry he was. "If you won't do it for yourself, Lori, do it for your baby."

Guilt slapped her in the face. Her baby had been suffering these past several weeks because she hadn't taken care of herself. She had to put her pride aside, had to remind herself that Gabe's solicitousness wasn't about her.

"I've spent so many years letting other people do everything for me. I'm afraid if I give in even once, I'll fall back into the same pattern."

His steady gaze on her softened, almost imperceptibly. "If I've learned one lesson, it's not to help people too much. You'll have to trust my judgment on this one."

She tried to push aside her emotions, to clearly see the right choice. But certainty, as usual, eluded her. "Okay. I can go along with that."

She followed him through the aisles as he filled the cart with food. First dry goods, then produce and dairy, then a few frozen items. He'd pause long enough to ask her if she liked red bell peppers or what kind of onions she preferred or whether she enjoyed a particular type of pasta. Then he'd add that item to the cart.

She tried insurrection once, insisting she didn't need both hot and cold cereal, but his pointed look silenced her. He scarcely allowed her to help, other than asking her to track down a foam cooler to keep the frozen goods in for the drive home. When she located the cooler, it was shelved above her reach and she had to call him to get it down.

As the checker rang up the purchases, she didn't even want to see the total. She forced herself to—knowing she had to know what she owed him. When the final number flashed on the register display, she gulped, then wrote it down on a scrap of paper in her purse.

He pushed the cart out the store and to the truck, his earlier tension dissipated. As he loaded the bags in the bed, he handed over the frozen items and she tucked them in with the ice in the cooler.

He handed her up into the truck again and Lori had her wallet ready when he got in. "Here's the first ten."

The money in her hand might as well have been a snake, the way he looked down at it. "I don't need it."

"You're getting it." She took his hand from the wheel and plunked the bill into it. "I told you I'm paying you back."

He folded his hand around the ten, and looked ready to give it back. Sitting straighter, she put as much steel as she could into her voice. "I won't take it back, Gabe."

He nodded then and shoved the money into his jeans pocket. "Fine."

"And I still owe you for gas."

He huffed out a sigh of exasperation. "I had to come down for supplies anyway, Lori. I probably saved the price of gas over what it would have cost me in Tahoe."

She was pretty sure the lumber wasn't that expensive up at the lake, but she figured it might be best to give in to the argument. Later, she could add the gas to what she owed.

"Okay." Her stomach rumbled and she put a hand over it. "I guess I ought to eat."

"We could stop for lunch." His thumb rapped out a staccato on the steering wheel. "But you might get car sick taking the curves on a full stomach."

Suddenly hunger roared through her. "I'm ravenous. I have to eat."

Pushing open the door, he slipped from the cab. When he returned, he had two hunks of French bread. "To tide you over."

He handed her a piece and she bit into the bread. "I've never tasted anything so good."

"Eat slowly. Wolf it down and you'll make yourself sick."

She smiled over at him. "Been around a lot of pregnant women, have you?"

About to take a bite of his own piece of bread, he stopped as pain washed over his face. He could have been a million miles away.

When he spoke, she barely heard the words. "I have a son."

He started the truck, revving the engine before backing from the parking space with a squeal. Wrenching the pickup into Drive, he took a breath, then pulled away more sedately.

They continued in silence down Carson Street, Lori nibbling on French bread, Gabe's piece in his lap. He obviously didn't want to say any more about his son, and as painful as it seemed to him, Lori would just as soon not press him. She had enough of her own secrets to conceal; she had no business prying into Gabe's past.

As they turned onto Highway 50, he picked up his bread and bit into it. "He's thirteen years old."

He didn't say another word the rest of the drive back.

When Gabe had left L.A., he'd left behind the only people who had known about Brandon. Other than Tyrell, he'd made a point of cutting off contact with that old life, at first too agonized to endure the reminders of his lost son, later unwilling to stir up the old, painful memories. Even his parents, whose hearts were just as shattered as his when Brandon disappeared, had stopped mentioning him in his presence.

Yet he had confessed his son's existence to Lori, when he could have just as easily sidestepped that revelation. He'd known other pregnant women besides his own ex-wife, had heard them complain endlessly about morning sickness and weird food cravings, could have brought them up as examples of his experience. But when Lori voiced her idle question, Brandon's face had leaped into his mind's eye and in that moment, denying his son's memory seemed like the ultimate betrayal.

The rest of the way back to the chalet, he'd kept his mouth shut, leaving well enough alone. That Lori respected his silence, that she didn't try to pry more of the story from him, filled him with a sense of grateful relief. He'd only managed to stay sane over the worst failure of his life by keeping it to himself. Not a soul in Hart Valley knew and he intended that situation to remain.

With a three-point turn, he backed the truck into the gravel drive, stopping with the bed close to the front steps. He knew Lori would insist on helping carry; he might as well make it as easy for her as possible.

He made sure the first bags he handed her were the lightest ones and once she'd gone inside, he quickly unloaded everything but the cooler, leaving the bags at the top of the stairs. By the time she'd returned, she had only to carry another light load straight to the house; the rest he took himself, three plastic bags in each hand.

She gave him a look when he set his load on the counter. "I'm not an invalid. I could have carried some of that."

He extricated the two half-gallon cartons of milk from one of the plastic bags. "Are you still hungry?"

"A little." Working alongside him, she unpacked bags into the pantry. "I could just have some more bread."

"I'll make you something after I bring in the cooler."

"You don't have to."

He counted to ten. "I have to eat anyway."

After he'd retrieved the cooler from the truck, he let her put away the frozen goods while he threw together sandwiches. He spiced up the bland lunch meat with a swipe of mustard, then added lettuce and slices of tomato. When he remembered how the acidity of tomato had turned Krista's stomach, he filched the slices from Lori's sandwich and added them to his.

They finished their respective tasks at the same time, Lori putting away the last of the dry goods just as he set the plates on the breakfast bar. Lori sank onto the stool with a sigh, eyeing her sandwich with genuine appetite.

"Thanks," she told him before taking a bite.

"This is how we'll do it." He tugged out a stool for himself. "I'll prepare the food, you clean up. I don't want to hear another word about it."

He expected her to protest, but she surprised him with a smile. It had its usual effect, punching him in the midsection with its force, sending heat low in his body.

She nodded, her smile changing to a beguiling curve of her mouth. "Yes, sir."

He ate his sandwich and didn't taste a single bite.

Either Gabe was a miracle worker or her body had finally thrown in the towel and decided it would cooperate with her pregnancy. She followed his advice, ate what he prepared for her, cleaned up afterward and experienced only occasional mild nausea she could easily head off with a few crackers. She slept better the next two nights as well, although her dreams were of a decidedly erotic nature, not particularly becoming for an expectant mother.

That was the downside to the end of her nausea—she had nothing to distract her from her still-tempting awareness of Gabe. With any luck her car would be repaired before she succumbed to that temptation.

Drying the last of the breakfast dishes and putting them away, Lori hung up the kitchen towel and grabbed her cell phone. She tucked it into her front pocket as she slipped out the back door. Amy had been out of town the past couple of days, but would be calling her later this morning and Lori didn't want to miss it.

Outside, she stopped and listened for Gabe. It had taken some serious arm-twisting yesterday, but he'd finally relented and let her help him with the deck repairs. He'd limited her role to switching out drill bits and keeping deck screws handy as he asked for them, but she'd enjoyed the time with him and the feeling of doing something useful.

She heard the whine of the drill from the south side of the chalet and turned toward the sound. After working on several smaller problem spots on the deck, Gabe had gone back to repairing the worst of the dry rot. She hadn't checked out the damage since the day she'd fallen and it took her a moment to work up her nerve to turn the corner and look.

She hesitated there as she surveyed the stretch of broken decking. Gabe was in the middle of it, working. He had his back to her as he fit a piece of redwood into place, the muscles of his shoulders working as he drove home the screws. She fought the urge to move up behind him, to put her hands on him, to feel the play of muscles against her palm.

"Hey," she said softly.

He looked over his shoulder at her. "Watch your step. Stay close to the house."

She did as instructed, keeping her feet within the safety zone as she approached. The box of deck screws sat out of his reach; he had two in his mouth. Once he'd driven those in, she had three more ready for him.

He took them from her. "How's the stomach?"

"Fine. I'm hoping I'm past the danger zone."

"Krista was sick four straight months." He mumbled the words around the screws, then looked as if he wished he hadn't said them at all.

"Your wife."

"Ex." He spat out the syllable as if it tasted evil in his mouth. "Hand me that piece of wood."

She grabbed the four-foot length of redwood and leaned to hold it within his reach. The cell phone dug into her leg and when she sat back again, she tugged it out and set it on the deck.

"Your son lives with her, then?"

The tendons on the back of his hand popped out in rigid lines as he gripped the two-by-six she'd given him. He held himself so stiffly, the muscles of his shoulders could have been made of iron.

He got to his feet, the piece of wood still in his hand, his chest heaving as he gasped in a breath. The two-by-six trembled so roughly she thought he'd drop it. Turning away with a roar fueled by some inner rage, he flung the length of redwood away and the piece sailed end over end in a slicing arc off into the trees.

His hands opening and closing into fists, he stared down at her, face wild, his green gaze lost in desolation. Then he turned away and stumbled across the deck to the rail, every line of his body screaming with agony. Lori's heart split in two seeing his pain and she pushed herself up, resting her palm against the wall of the house when she felt a moment of light-headedness.

Picking her path carefully, she moved up behind him, and put her hand on the iron muscles of his back. As she stroked from side to side, he seemed oblivious to her presence, too lost to her. Then he turned, and with a look of desperation, cupped his hands on her shoulders. He pulled her closer, his head tipping down to hers.

Chapter Eleven

She could feel his need transmitted through his touch, his harsh breathing, the heat that increased as he urged her closer. In the back of her mind, she knew she should pull away, knew she'd be a fool to let him kiss her, to let the fire burn any brighter between them.

But his passion stroked along her nerve endings, burrowed deep inside her, lighting an answering flame she couldn't deny. As wrong as she knew it was, she had to kiss him, had to feel his mouth on hers.

The first touch of his lips nearly brought her to tears. A mix of tenderness edged with fever, the contact reached so deep inside her, he might as well have climbed into her heart. When she would have expected his raging pain to translate into roughness, instead he sipped at her mouth, the tautness of his arms where her fingers curled around them the only sign of his tension.

He wanted her. The message screamed along her veins, accelerating her heart. He wanted her and she wanted him with a desperation she hadn't the strength to deny.

His mouth covered hers more fully, his hand moving behind her head to release her hair from the barrette she'd used to pull it back. His fingers dove into her loosened hair as his tongue dipped just past her lips, moving along the seam, easing her mouth open.

His tongue slipping alongside hers sent a shot of sensation through her. She moved her hands up his arms to his shoulders, still feeling the tension there, then curved one around the back of his neck. While his fingers moved in a mesmerizing pattern in her hair, she clung to him, her knees growing so weak she thought she'd sink to the deck.

He turned her toward the rail, pressing his lower body against hers, the hard ridge of his raised flesh impossible to ignore. She wanted to wrap herself around him, draw him deep inside her, feel the force of his potency driving into her. The instant escalation from a simple kiss to the compulsive need burning inside her shocked her with its power.

His hand had drifted down her arm, down her side, to her waist. He took a handful of the knit of her T-shirt and freed it from her jeans, his fingers then dipping underneath. He traced a lazy path along her rib cage, the gentle pressure forcing the air from her lungs. Then his thumb grazed the underside of her breast and a soft moan escaped from her, the sound swallowed by Gabe's kiss.

Turning her away from the rail, he guided her backward toward the house, his relentless kisses stealing her will. Halfway there, he reached behind to release her bra, exquisitely careful with the healing scrapes on her back. His hand closed around her breast, full and aching with pleasure and she couldn't hold back another moan.

Her fingers dug into his shoulders as he ran his palm back and forth across her tight nipple. He must have known how tender her breasts were from her pregnancy, how it would hurt if he manhandled her. His touch was incredibly gentle, featherlight, and all the more erotic to her oversensitized flesh.

He'd edged her toward the back door, had one hand on the knob when she heard the bleat of her cell phone. It didn't register at first, its shrill call an annoyance her body told her to disregard. But with its second ring, Gabe backed away, took his hands from her, staring down at her, dazed.

"Should get that," he muttered.

She could only nod, incapable of speech. He moved slowly to where she'd left the phone, one hand on the wall for support as he bent to pick it up.

He pressed the answer button. "Hello?" he barked into the phone, his harsh greeting that of a man interrupted from lovemaking. Lori could only imagine what Amy would make of it.

Gabe's eyes narrowed. "Who is *this*?"

Lori wouldn't have expected a grilling from Amy, the quintessential diplomat. Her sponsor would save the inquisition for Lori.

"Yes," Gabe ground out, flicking a glance up at her. "She's here."

He covered the phone's mouthpiece. "A man. For you. He wouldn't give his name."

Lori's heart sank to her toes. Hugh wouldn't have called her here, couldn't in fact since she'd changed her cell service after he took a powder. Only one man had this number.

Lori held out her hand for the phone and Gabe

gave it to her. She glanced at the caller ID to confirm the caller, then lifted it to her ear.

"Hello, Tom."

The phone call was a lifesaver. His body was still primed and ready for Lori, would have had her on the sofa, her bed or his by now if the cell hadn't intervened. While his logical, sensible side was relieved, his carnal side wanted another go-round with her.

The caller had been plenty pissed to hear Gabe's voice answering instead of Lori's. It hadn't seemed like a proprietary anger—not the self-righteousness of a jealous boyfriend. The man had been as unwilling as Gabe to identify himself, so Gabe had no clue to the man's relationship to Lori.

He could see the tension in her face as she spoke in low, clipped tones to the man she'd called Tom. A brother, maybe? He didn't know much about the Hightower family; was there a brother? Considering Lori's financial situation, she must not be in close contact with her parents; maybe this brother was an emissary whose mission it was to bring her back into the fold.

Looking off into the trees, he considered whether to retrieve the piece he'd thrown or just cut another. The overwhelming rage that had driven him to heave it into the surrounding pines had receded back behind the walls that usually confined it. The length of redwood was just a mute piece of lumber with no more significance than any of the other pieces he'd fitted into the deck.

But there was a kernel of Krista in that bit of two-by-six, a fragment of her treachery, her horrific betrayal. Part of him would just as soon throw the piece into a shredder and burn the resulting chips. If only by doing so he could magically change what had happened ten years ago, could bring the past decade onto the proper track so that instead of despair he would have had a life with his son.

Lori's voice changed as she spoke and from her softer, sweeter tone, he could tell she was speaking to a child. Her niece, maybe? She'd turned away from him so he could only catch part of what Lori was saying—an apology for not having called, questions about school. Lori glanced over her shoulder at Gabe, making him acutely aware that he was eavesdropping. Deciding he could use a cola, he turned and headed into the house.

Standing in the kitchen with the icy can in his hand, thoughts of his son rolled over him. He would have thought he was finished with torturing himself with might-have-beens. But somehow, his encounter with Lori on the deck stirred up the impossible what-ifs—what if things had been different between him and Krista? What if she'd been a different kind of woman, had been able to communicate to him that she couldn't handle their marriage?

They could have divorced before she left, could have worked out a shared custody agreement. He could have had the past ten years with his son. It wouldn't have been ideal for Brandon, spending one week at his mother's home, then the next at his father's. Especially at first, as young as Brandon was it would be hard to understand. But wouldn't that have been better than spending ten years without his dad, without knowing why his father didn't come to see him anymore?

Claws of grief dug into his belly as they always did when he ventured down the forbidden path of wishful thinking. He had to get back to work, give his mind something to do instead of dwelling on the old, dead past.

He'd just turned toward the door when it opened and Lori hurried inside. He thought at first she'd been overcome by another bout of nausea, but she didn't head for the bathroom. She half ran past him into the great room, straight for the wet bar and the liquor cabinet above it.

Setting aside his soda, he followed her, stopping a few feet behind her. She yanked open the cabinet and grabbed the nearest bottle—scotch whiskey. One hand on the lid, she hesitated, then pulled a highball glass from the shelf.

Her hand shook as she set down the tumbler, the clatter of glass against tile jarring in the quiet room. Another hesitation before she unscrewed the lid of the bottle of scotch and lifted it with a shaking hand.

She didn't pour, didn't even tip the bottle. She just stared down at the glass, her slender shoulders hunched in misery, anguish clear in every line of her body.

When she picked up the bottle lid, her hand was steady. Closing it tight, she put the scotch back in the cabinet, then shut the door again. Tugging on the cold water at the sink, she filled the highball glass with water, then turned to face Gabe.

He gave her another minute to compose herself, then asked, "You want to talk about it?"

Her gaze dropped to the water in her hands. She took another swallow. "The man you spoke to...that was my ex-husband, Tom."

That explained the third degree. "And after you spoke to him…"

"That was my daughter. Jessie."

The revelation rocked him. He wasn't sure why. He knew so little about her; it shouldn't surprise him she had a past that included a child.

Envy ate at him. She had a child, spoke to her, knew where she lived. He would give his right arm for that privilege with Brandon.

He pushed aside the roiling emotions. "Your ex-husband has custody?"

Pain flashed across her face. "Yes."

"Because of your drinking?"

She looked away, her grip tightening on the glass. "Partly."

"You've cleaned up your act this past year. I would think you could get some sort of shared custody."

She still wouldn't look at him. "It's more complicated than that."

"Complicated enough to make you desperate for a drink?"

Setting aside her glass of water, she faced him. "Tom wasn't awarded custody because I'm an alcoholic. It was because I deserted him. And I abandoned my daughter."

At first Gabe thought he hadn't heard her right. "Abandoned…I don't understand."

She crossed her arms over her middle and leaned against the wet bar. "Six years ago, I walked out. Left Tom and Jessie behind. Was almost completely out of her life until I quit drinking."

Even as she said the words, Gabe could barely grasp them. Ten years of agony without his son, and this woman just walked away from her daughter? Tears filled Lori's eyes, but Gabe wouldn't let himself feel even an iota of sympathy.

"Now, she doesn't want to have anything to do with me." She hugged herself tighter. "She doesn't want me coming for her birthday, says I'll ruin everything."

"Do you blame her?" The words came out harshly, sharp with an anger he didn't try to conceal.

"Of course not!" Her ire matched his own. "Of course I don't blame her. They were *my* mistakes, not hers. I don't intend to force a relationship on her. I want one…" Her tears choked her words. "Want one so badly. Want her to love me. But how can she?"

Even as he tried to absorb what Lori had told him, a thought hit him with hurricane force. What if Krista somehow realized the enormity of her transgression, brought Brandon back to him, asked his forgiveness? Would he waste time and energy hating his ex-wife? Or would he simply rejoice at having his son back in his life?

At least Lori had acknowledged her mistake, took responsibility for the pain she'd given her daughter. Who was he to judge her?

But she'd walked away from her daughter!

Lori's serious brown gaze fixed on him. "A few days ago, I asked you about forgiveness. You said some sins can never be washed away. Do you think this is one of them?"

Yes! came immediately to mind, but he bit it back. "That's between you and your daughter."

She nodded, accepting his answer. "She has a stepmother now—Andrea. She's a good woman. I know she loves my daughter."

He'd never let himself consider that Krista had remarried, that Brandon might have grown up calling another man Daddy. The possibility cut too deep to even think about. Easier to focus on Lori and what she was saying.

"I can tell by the way Jessie talks about Andrea…" Her voice trailed off and he could hear the pain. "Jessie loves her very much. It hurts, but…I'm so glad she has someone to be a mother to her."

Taking the glass, she emptied it down the sink, then carried it to the kitchen. She stood there, glass in her hand, as if not sure what to do next.

"I have to get back to work." He moved toward the back door.

"I deserve it. Your judgment."

His hand on the door, he didn't look at her. "I'm not your jury."

He heard the *clunk* as she set the glass on the counter. "Leaving Jessie was the biggest mistake of my life. But at the same time, I was the worst mother in the world for her."

"That doesn't excuse it."

"Nothing does." Her voice was bleak. "Nothing will. Certainly not a glass of scotch."

There was nothing he could say to that. He turned the knob, stepped outside.

As he breathed in the scent of pine, he wanted to hold on to his anger, to use it as a defense against her. He already felt inexplicably tied to her, partly because of his unrelenting attraction to her, but also because he understood her wounds, felt them in his own soul. Her abandonment of her daughter didn't jibe with the woman he thought he was beginning to know. But who knew what demons haunted her past?

Damnably, he wanted her to follow him out the door, to work alongside him as she had been. He'd become accustomed to having her with him, an arm's length away, close enough to catch her fragrance, near enough to touch the silk of her hair.

As he followed the lazy circles of a red-tailed hawk high above the lake, he forced himself to admit the truth. He wanted her closer than arm's length. He wanted her skin to skin, him deep inside her, her legs tangled with his.

How had he come to need her, burn for her so intensely in only a few days? Because he'd come to such a low point before he arrived here, the last elusive clues to Brandon's whereabouts spent, his hopes of finding his son nearly drowned? Because he simply needed comfort, and any woman's ease would have done? Or because the dark nights of her soul so closely mirrored his own and only she could drag him to the light?

He couldn't bring himself to return to his work, even as the guilt lay heavily on him that he ought to be doing what he'd committed to Tyrell to do. Without thought or consideration of where he was going, he headed for the stairs and down them, then into the thick pines and cedars, along the narrow deer trail. He wanted nothing more than to go back inside and be with Lori—which was exactly why he had to leave.

His work boots skidded and slid down the rocky hillside as he scrambled down toward the lake. He didn't know where he was going or what he would do when he got there. There was only one certainty—he might for the moment escape the emotions Lori stirred inside him, but he would never outrun his ghosts.

Gabe's reaction to the sins of her past had been no worse than she'd expected. It shouldn't hurt as much as it did, but then he shouldn't have become as important to her as he had so that his opinion of her mattered so much.

As it was, she'd left out the most damning part of her story, still had that revelation to look forward to if she decided to be completely up front with him. But why would she need to when he would walk out of her life in such a few short days?

She recalled the rage with which he had hurled that piece of two-by-six into the trees. He had a son, a boy just a couple of years older than Jessie. She didn't know what had goaded him to express his rage that way—estrangement from his ex-wife, his son or maybe both. But whatever truth Gabe hid behind the layers and walls he used to protect himself, it likely wouldn't make him any more accepting of the worst of her transgressions with Jessie.

When Lori had reached the eighth of the twelve steps, her daughter had topped the list of those people she had harmed. She'd stalled on the ninth step— making amends—because she couldn't resolve in her own heart whether her presence in Jessie's life would heal or hurt her daughter.

Gabe had left the back door open when he'd stepped outside, an action that seemed to symbolize what she longed for with her daughter—permission to reenter her life. Lori couldn't ask for it, couldn't expect it. She could only pray that someday her daughter would be willing to say yes.

Folded in the bottom of her suitcase, a little rumpled from having been there for several weeks, was a letter. She had written and rewritten it over and over, trying to choose exactly the right words, frame the emotions inscribed in her heart clearly so her daughter would understand. She'd stripped away anything that smacked of self-pity, had laid every blame and fault on herself. Her goal had been only to open the door she'd slammed shut six years ago, to open it as wide as possible and leave the choice to her daughter as to whether to step through.

But the letter still lay in her suitcase, tucked into an envelope addressed to her daughter. Her struggle to make amends lacked only one necessary action—putting the stamped envelope in the mail.

A sudden urgency to send the letter washed over her. It seemed imperative she not wait another moment. The sooner Jessie read it, the sooner they might rebuild what Lori had destroyed six years ago.

When she'd walked down the access road the other day, she'd seen the bank of locked mailboxes near the highway. There was a slot at the top to drop outgoing mail. The letter could go out today if the carrier hadn't already picked up, tomorrow at the latest.

Hurrying into the bedroom, she tugged her suitcase out from under the bed and unzipped it. She hadn't sealed the envelope yet, leaving herself the option of rewriting the letter again. But it was time to commit herself. She'd expressed her feelings about as well as she ever would. She couldn't allow her fear of her daughter's response delay her from sending the letter any longer.

She read it through quickly, only adding at the bottom, *With all my love, Mom.* Licking the flap, she pressed it shut and ran her thumb over it to be sure it was closed. Then she hurried out the front door and down the steps.

A tree root brought an end to his headlong rush down the hill, the loop of cedar catching his foot and sending him sprawling into a manzanita. The shock of sharp manzanita branches strafing his palms yanked him from the darkness that had driven him from the chalet, as effective as a slap to the face.

He leaned back against a nearby cedar to catch his breath and assess the damage to his hands. They were scraped, the angry scratches dotted with blood. A sliver of red manzanita had broken off and embedded itself at the base of his thumb on his right hand. It was in too deep to easily remove without tweezers.

A sound drifted down the hillside—was it Lori calling him? He started back up the hill, the deer trail barely discernible through the underbrush. He thought he heard Lori again, but the breeze seemed to brush away the sound.

Quickening his pace, he scrambled through the manzanita and pine, occasionally slapping a hand on a tree or boulder for balance, then wincing at the tenderness of his palm. His heart hammered in his chest as he imagined all the horrible possibilities, the reasons Lori might be calling him.

"Gabe!" Her voice was loud enough now to hear clearly and he tried to detect panic in her call, fear.

He couldn't see her yet through the thick trees and brush, had no way of knowing if she was hurt.

A stitch in his side forced him to stop. An elbow against a white fir, he gasped in breath. "Lori?"

"Gabe? Are you okay?"

If she was in distress, it didn't show in her voice. Pushing off, he continued steadily up the deer trail until he reached the clearing around the chalet. Lori stood several yards away, at the well-marked trailhead.

When she saw him, she jumped back, startled. "You didn't take the trail."

His hands were throbbing in earnest now and he clutched them into fists. "What did you want?"

"I was just wondering where you were. I took a walk up the road to mail a letter."

He closed the distance between them. "I should have gone with you."

"I was fine by myself."

"You'd be safer with me."

Her dark eyes snapped with anger. "I didn't want to inconvenience you."

"It would be more of an inconvenience if you'd passed out on the road." He flung his hand out in irritation.

She grabbed his wrist. "What did you do to yourself?"

"It's nothing."

She uncurled his fingers, relentless. "Now who can't take care of themselves?" she murmured as she examined the bloody scrapes.

"I'll deal with it."

"Don't be an idiot. It's hard to doctor your own

hands." A gentle finger trailed down his thumb. "You'll need some help with that splinter." She turned and towed him toward the steps.

He felt like a three-year-old following his mommy, although there was nothing maternal in the sensations her touch evoked. "I don't need your help." He tried to pull free as they crossed the deck toward the back door, but her grip was surprisingly strong.

"Indulge me. I need the practice."

She left him in the kitchen, then headed for her bedroom, no doubt to retrieve the first aid kit. He washed his hands at the kitchen sink, sucking in a breath when the liquid soap stung his wounds. Once the blood was gone, he saw his scrapes were minor, the sliver of manzanita wedged under the skin the worst of it.

He was dabbing his hands dry with a paper towel when she returned with the plastic box. "I saw a pair of tweezers in here." Opening the lid, she bent her head to search.

Nudging her aside, he lifted the top tray aside and located the tweezers. She put her hand out for them. He didn't want to relinquish them, didn't want his hand nestled in hers as she pulled the splinter free. The crazy flood of emotions the last hour had battered down barriers inside him, barricades he needed time to rebuild. In that moment, he felt so sensitized, he didn't know if he could control his responses to her.

"Are you left-handed?" she asked. He shook his head, mesmerized by the motion her mouth made as she spoke. She took the tweezers from him. "Then you'll have a heck of a time getting that splinter out of your right hand."

Her warm fingers wrapped around his wrist and the

back of his hand rested against the tender skin of her inner arm. She spread his fingers aside, the act impossibly erotic. He didn't even feel the tweezers poking and prodding as she maneuvered to get a grip on the thin shard of manzanita. His senses were too full of the sight of her silky blond head bent down to her task, the sensation of her hand cradling his.

When she'd gotten the splinter free of his thumb and set aside the tweezers, her hand trembled and she kept her gaze downcast. When she would have let him go and backed away, he curved his hands around her upper arms and kept her close. Energy burned between them, so charged it obliterated his awareness of anything else in the room.

His palm against her face, he tipped her head back. The fire in her eyes brought him immediately to the boiling point. He wanted everything at once—to kiss her, to see her pale skin under his hands, to touch her everywhere. He would die if he didn't press his mouth against hers that instant.

"Say no," he whispered harshly. "Say it now."

Her lips parted, her pulse beat rapidly in her throat. "I won't say no."

He stared at her a moment longer, looking for any sign of unwillingness, anything to pull him off this path. He saw only heat, he saw only desire.

He lowered his mouth to hers.

Chapter Twelve

As Gabe's mouth covered hers, Lori tried to muster reason, some justification for stopping him. But she felt nothing but the touch of his lips brushing hers, the moist graze of his tongue along her mouth, then dipping inside.

He pressed her against the kitchen counter, one hand spread across the small of her back, the other at her jaw, his thumb stroking her cheek. Her fingers curled along his sides, feeling the play of muscles under his T-shirt, the heat of him soaking into her. She felt desperate to get his shirt off and her own, to feel his skin next to hers.

He hesitated, drawing back a fraction. "Last chance. Say no."

"I want you," was the only response she gave.

He lifted her then, high enough to let her wrap her legs around him, his hand supporting her hips. Kissing her as he went, he carried her to the master bedroom, through the door. Shutting it behind him, he closed them inside the dim coolness, the privacy of the room, of the chalet itself, heightening the intimacy.

Lowering her to the bed, he knelt to slip off her

sneakers, then pushed his feet out of his own. He urged her back onto the bed, but he didn't undress her or himself. He stared down at her, his intense green gaze raking her from head to toe, his chest heaving, his body taut with tension.

"You're almost too beautiful."

She smiled, nervous, too aroused to think clearly. He dropped to one knee and brushed his lips against hers. "When you smile, you're beyond beautiful."

She felt tears prick her eyes. "Sometimes I've hated my looks."

She expected the usual response—disbelief that anyone could regret such a wonderful gift. But she should have known better than to expect the usual from Gabe.

"People see your face and they make judgments about you." Cradling her face with his hands, he trailed kisses across her face. "Assume things."

That he understood seemed an incomparable blessing. "And what's your judgment of me?"

He drew back. "I don't like the choices you made."

"I don't either, but I made them."

"I shouldn't like you, shouldn't want you."

"Then walk away."

Her heart seemed to stop as he stared down at her, the faint light in the room painting shadows on his face. A part of her realized it would be better if he left, but another corner of her soul knew that would tear her apart.

He rose and she was sure he was about to leave the room. Instead he lay down beside her, his body against hers from head to toe. "I don't know what's right anymore," he murmured, his mouth moving against her throat, "or what's wrong."

In his embrace, nothing felt wrong. He slipped one leg between hers, bringing her leg up to his hip. She felt his hard flesh against the V of her legs, the sensation setting her heart to pounding. They lay there fully dressed, yet she thought she might reach climax just from the closeness.

His tongue traced the whorls of her ear, his unsteady breathing tightening the knot of excitement even further. Her hand stroked his back, reveling in the feel of muscle, of heat through his knit shirt.

She felt his fingers in her hair, felt him draw them across her sensitive scalp. He brought the fall of hair to his face, breathed in the fragrance, burrowed in the silky locks.

"I've wanted to do this since the first day I met you."

His fingers still woven in her hair, he drew his mouth from her ear along the line of her jaw, to her throat, lingering on the pulse point there. With his leg pressing between hers, his heavy flesh against the most sensitive part of her, she felt dangerously close to the edge.

It hadn't been this way with other men. She'd rarely found pleasure in the act, had been so desperate for some kind of fulfillment, she almost never reached it. Tom had been a tender, caring lover, but not even he could break through the wall the sense of worthlessness had built.

But the barest touch of Gabe's mouth, his hands, his body excited her beyond what she would have thought capable. She shook all over just from the realization.

Still kissing her, he tugged her T-shirt free of her

jeans, dragging it higher. She shifted to allow him to pull it over her head and the coolness of the room on her heated skin only added to the edge of desire.

One finger stroking lightly along the strap of her utilitarian white maternity bra, he gazed down at her. "Are they sore?"

"Sensitive," she gasped as he drew his finger over one breast. Her nipple immediately beaded under his touch.

"I'll be careful." He reached behind her, unhooking the bra, then lowering the straps, one by one. She waited for him to put his hands on her, was certain just that contact would bring her to climax. But then he leaned his head down and brushed his lips ever so gently against one beaded tip.

She couldn't hold back a moan, her hands clutching at his shoulders. She couldn't lie still either, her hips restless under him.

"Am I hurting you?" His voice was rough with need.

"No. It feels…"

His tongue lapped her again and she moaned, the sound vibrating low in her body. She grabbed handfuls of his shirt, wanting it off him, wanting to feel him against her.

He arched up off the bed and pulled the shirt off himself, throwing it aside. She reached for the button of his jeans, but he pushed her hands away. "Not yet."

He wasn't above unsnapping her jeans and tugging down the zipper. She gasped as his fingers parted the zipper and brushed against her panties. "No fair."

"To hell with fair." He peeled her jeans down her hips, then slid them off. "Not much has been fair in my life."

Moving up beside her again, he cupped her through her panties, fingers pressing against the dampness between her legs. He pulled a nipple into his mouth, sucking gently.

"Definitely not fair," she managed, feeling the heat rise even higher. Her hips pushed at his hand of their own accord.

With slow deliberation, still drawing the heated tip of her breast into his mouth, his hand moved up to the top of her panties. His fingers dipped underneath the elastic band, then made a leisurely trail down to the curls between her legs.

As his fingers parted the curls, he put his mouth on hers, his tongue diving inside just as his finger slipped inside her. His palm pushing aside her folds to press against the nub at the apex, his tongue thrust in rhythm with his finger. She didn't have a chance.

At the first powerful wave rushing through her body, she cried out, the sound swallowed by his intimate kiss. Another crest hit on the heels of the first, driven from her body by Gabe's expert touch. With a shock, she peaked a third time, sensation drowning her in pleasure.

As she trembled in the aftermath, his hand still on her, his mouth now sipping at hers, she stared shell-shocked at the ceiling. Tears spilled from the corners of her eyes, but it wasn't grief she felt. It was wonder.

He lifted his head, a faint smile on his face. Wiping the tears away with his thumb, he cupped her cheek. "Okay?"

"More than. But I want…" She pushed at his jeans.

He levered away from her and stripped away his

jeans and shorts. As he lay back on the bed, she put out a hand to stop him. "Do you have protection?"

"Yes."

She tried a smile, but it felt stiff on her face. "You can't make me any more pregnant, but the way my life used to be...I just want to be sure *you're* protected."

His expression didn't change, but he picked up his jeans and pulled out a foil square. Once he'd sheathed himself, he lay back down and urged her legs apart.

His hand resting lightly on her thigh, he hesitated. "This doesn't mean commitment."

An ache centered in her heart. "No strings," she agreed, although strings were exactly what she longed for.

His green gaze burned into her. "No strings." He said it matter-of-factly, but her yearning heart thought it heard a trace of regret.

Then he pushed between her legs with a slow, confident stroke and she forgot about everything but the feel of him inside her. She locked her heels at the small of his back, drawing him as deep as she could, then gave herself over to him. He thrust inside as his gaze riveted on hers, the power of his lovemaking rocking the foundations of her world.

This was beyond what she'd ever felt with a man, in an entirely different universe. This wasn't just bodies moving together, this was sensation distilled, emotion purified into the most glorious treasure. To say she cared for him was too pallid, too meaningless. Her feelings in that moment went beyond simple caring.

She loved him.

The realization shocked her as surely as her climax, both hitting her so hard she threw back her head as if from a blow, eyes shut tight. As she felt his body tighten with his own completion, wave after wave of pleasure crashed over her, love and passion mixed in magnificent splendor, shaking her to the core. She wouldn't come back from this experience the same person, had been transformed by the power of their union.

She was terrified to open her eyes again, almost more afraid of what she might see than of what he would. She didn't expect any answering love. But she prayed there wouldn't be indifference.

Stunned by what had just happened, Gabe buried his face against Lori's neck and tried to work out how to put the world back on its foundations. This interlude with Lori—hell, how could he simply call it an interlude?—this *experience* went beyond any other in his life. Krista wasn't so much as a pale imitation, and his times with other women didn't even come close.

He could be dishonest and just call it sex, incredibly mind-blowing pleasure. But Lori had reached inside him during those white-hot moments, and a part of her still lingered there. He didn't know if he could ever dislodge her.

What the hell was he going to do now? Just get up from the bed, say "thank you very much," and go on with his life? He wasn't sure he could even put two words together yet, with his mental capacities exploded by a climax to beat all climaxes.

He raised his head, a little worried about what she might see in his face. When she met his gaze, she seemed a little wary, as if wondering herself about what came next.

"I need to clean up," he told her, amazed at the blush painting her cheeks.

He didn't want to move, but he edged away. As he rose from the bed, a weight started filling his chest where his heart should be. He didn't know what he'd expected from her, what he wanted from her. His mind seemed to have stopped functioning entirely, leaving only unfamiliar emotions to stew inside him.

Staring at himself in the bathroom mirror, he felt too damn vulnerable. Maybe she'd just gather up the clothes scattered on the floor and bed, get dressed and leave the bedroom. He would have thought that would make it easier, but imagining her gone from the bed when he stepped from the bathroom just added to the heaviness inside him.

When he returned to the bedroom, Lori's mouth curved in a gentle smile and the tension inside him eased. She leaned against the headboard, the comforter tucked up to cover her incredible breasts, her expression becoming serious.

"I have to talk to you, Gabe. Tell you something."

For a crazy moment, he thought she might tell him she loved him and his heart skyrocketed to the heavens. Why he'd want that, when he didn't love her, he didn't understand. He tamped down the mixed-up feelings, sliding into the bed beside her.

"What I told you about leaving Jessie, what really happened—it's bad, Gabe."

He took her hand. "Tell me."

She curled her fingers in his, her gaze downcast. "There was an accident. Jessie hurt herself. I should have been watching her, but instead…" Tears poured down her face, but she wiped them away impatiently.

"I was otherwise occupied," she said bitterly. "When I should have been there to protect my child."

Just as he should have protected Brandon from Krista, should have somehow seen the signs. "What happened?"

"Tom was on a horse-buying trip. I…I'd gotten pretty cozy with the ranch foreman." Head lifted, she faced him squarely. "There was a power outage around midnight. I was in the foreman's apartment."

Her lips pressed tight, he could see the self-recrimination in her face. "Jessie woke up, scared of the dark. The flashlight wouldn't work so she lit a candle. I didn't even know what happened until she screamed…."

The horror of it gripped Gabe. What if something like that had happened to Brandon since he'd been with Krista? As crazy as she'd been just before she'd left, Gabe didn't know if his ex-wife would have had the presence of mind to help Brandon if he was hurt. All these years imagining Brandon whole, healthy, happy could just be an illusion. That tore at him.

"Tom was just pulling up when she ran out of the house, the sleeve of her sweatshirt on fire. God, she looked so terrified." She didn't bother wiping away the tears. "By the time we put out the flames, she'd been badly burned. I rode with her to the hospital, then…"

She took in a ragged breath. "You know, failure is the only thing I've ever done well. And my daughter paid the price."

She scrubbed at her face with the heels of her hands. "I hung in there for six months, during the worst of Jessie's recovery. Overwhelmed by guilt, with remorse. One night as I left the hospital, it hit me—having no mother would be better for Jessie than having a mother like me."

"So you gave up. Walked away."

"Yes. Yet another wrong choice in a lifetime of wrong choices."

She pushed from the bed, keeping her back to him as she found her clothes and struggled into them. "She has Andrea now. A real mother. I'm just an awkward embarrassment to her." Half-dressed, shoes in one hand, jeans in the other, she hurried from the room.

Compassion pierced his heart, and he ached to shelter her from the pain. But he couldn't wrap his mind around this last bit of damning evidence against Lori. Yet if he somehow found Brandon, got him back, wouldn't he do everything he could to keep Krista out of his son's life forever? It wouldn't matter to him that she was Brandon's mother.

That bitter pill didn't sit well inside him. He rose, pulling on clothes quickly. When he stepped into the great room, Lori was tying her shoes. "I'm going for a walk."

He pushed bare feet into his sneakers, his socks still lost somewhere in the bedroom. "What do you want from me?"

She wouldn't look up at him as she rose. "Nothing." She slammed the front door on her way out.

Leaving his laces untied, he followed her without thinking, catching up on the gravel drive. "I should hate you, hate everything about you."

She walked faster. "Feel free."

He kept pace with her easily. "I don't. I want to,

but I don't. You haven't asked me to understand, expected me to forgive."

She turned to him, her eyes snapping with anger. "It's not your place to forgive me."

"I don't know how to forgive." An answering anger rose in him, but not directed at Lori. "She took him. In the dead of night, without a word of warning. Took him out of his bed."

The despair, the white-hot rage exploded inside him. Grabbing up handfuls of the gravel at his feet, he hurled them into the trees, wishing the pebbles were larger so they'd break something. Instead they bounced off the tall ponderosas and tumbled into the underbrush.

He felt his knees give out, couldn't stand anymore. He sank to the rough driveway and buried his face in his hands.

When he first felt her cool touch, he thought he'd lose it, thought the sobs would rip from his throat the way they had that dark night Krista had taken Brandon. She took his hand and urged him to his feet, her arms encircling him, her sweet warm body against his.

He shook as he held onto her so tight he was afraid he'd hurt her. She pulled away and took his hand again, guiding him to the front stairs. She sat down and tugged him down beside her.

"Tell me," she said softly.

He hadn't related the entire story since that horrible night ten years ago when he'd first reported Brandon's disappearance. He was sure the knot in his throat wouldn't let him do it now.

But her touch eased the tightness inside him and

he found he could speak. "My marriage to Krista was never—" he groped for the words "—never quite right."

Lori stroked his back, her steadiness a comfort. "Where did you meet her?"

"A bar. A place where cops hung out after their shifts. She was at a corner table drinking a soda."

He remembered his first glimpse of her, the sweet innocence of her blue eyes, her light brown hair pulled back on either side with barrettes. She'd seemed barely old enough to be in a bar at all. If he'd known the history behind that guileless face, he would have never crossed the room to say hello.

"We talked all night. When the bar closed, we found a coffee shop. Somehow, we ended up at my place, in bed."

Over the years, he'd run it through his mind how their relationship had gone so far so fast. "A week later, she told me she loved me. A month after that, she announced she was pregnant."

That had completely knocked him off his feet. He'd had every intention of taking responsibility for the child Krista carried, so her suggestion of marriage should have seemed natural and exactly right. But even then, he sensed something amiss in Krista's sweet face.

"We had a quickie wedding in Vegas. A month later things started falling apart. Krista swung from one mood to the next, and I could barely keep up. I'd ask her what was wrong, but half the time, she wouldn't even speak to me."

"She was bipolar," Lori said softly.

He looked at her in surprise. "Yes."

"A cousin of mine has gone through that with her son. Did your wife stop taking her meds?"

"She was afraid she'd hurt the baby."

She'd finally confessed to him in the third trimester, begged him to hang in there with her, promised she'd resume her medications once the baby was born. He'd believed her, had toughed it out through the worst days, keeping on an even keel even when she couldn't.

"She kept her word at first," Gabe said, remembering. "Bottle-fed Brandon so she could resume the meds. Things were looking better. She seemed like a great mom. A little overprotective, a little paranoid about Brandon getting hurt. But I thought that was just because he was her first."

They limped through the next couple years, Gabe hoping his steady, dependable love for his child would make up for Krista's hot and cold swings. She never hurt Brandon, at least not physically. But when she slipped up with her medication regimen, she sometimes frightened Brandon, sending the little boy running for his father.

"When Brandon was two, I told Krista we had to hire a nanny. Krista wasn't working, but I wanted someone there when I was on patrol."

"She went along with that?"

"The doctor had finally gotten her dosage right and she was clearheaded enough to agree. And…" His stomach tightened. "I gave her an ultimatum. Either a nanny or I'd take Brandon from her."

The sun hung overhead, marking noontime. He ought to be hungry, ready for lunch, but the thought of eating just turned his stomach. He was too caught up in regrets—that he'd issued that ultimatum, that he hadn't seen sooner Krista's growing imbalance, that he'd ever crossed that bar to talk to her in the first place.

"When she said yes to the nanny, I assumed we were in agreement. I'd forgotten how good she was at hiding."

In his ignorance, the next year seemed nearly idyllic to him. He was on day shift and almost kept banker's hours. He'd come home to a dinner prepared by the nanny, say goodbye to the grandmotherly caregiver, then go looking for Brandon and Krista. Most days they were playing together happily, a perfect picture of motherly affection. The bad days were further and fewer between.

"I finally thought we'd make it as a couple. We wouldn't have any more kids—I couldn't risk overloading Krista with more stress. But I thought as long as we had the nanny and Krista continued with the meds, we were fine."

The rest of the story unreeled in his head, as vivid as a movie. "The night of July Fourth they pulled in extra patrols, me included. I arranged for the nanny to stay overnight. Found out later Krista had sent her home."

Even now, he didn't blame the older woman for leaving. Brandon was already in bed, Krista seemed stable. Gabe would be home in two hours.

"When I pulled up, every light in the house was on. I started calling for them the moment I stepped in the door. I ran to Brandon's room first…"

He could still see the empty bed, the rumpled covers, the special blanket Brandon dragged around with him everywhere cast aside on the floor. How many nights did his son cry for that blanket?

"I went to Krista's and my room next, praying she'd just taken him in there to sleep with her. That's when I saw the half-empty closet, the dresser drawers hanging open."

The images pounded into his brain, the emotions rolling through him all over again. He hunched over with the pain of it, only Lori's arm around him making the relentless ache bearable.

"She covered her tracks well. Her own parents didn't know where she went. The few clues she'd left didn't pan out. Over the years I've followed every lead I could find, hired private investigators when I hit a wall. Tyrell has helped me when he could, keeping me informed from L.A."

There was a wealth of sympathy in her soft brown eyes. "How long?"

"Ten years next month. Independence Day is always tough to get through."

"But you're still looking."

"Yes." The futility of his search dragged at him. "I can't let him go."

"Of course not."

He fixed his gaze on her. "He's lost, Lori. Completely lost to me."

She curved a hand around his cheek. "There's got to be a way to find him."

"I've tried them all." Bitterness settled deep inside him. "He may not even be alive anymore."

"Gabe…"

Her gentle voice should have soothed him, but it only made the pain sharper. He couldn't talk about it anymore, couldn't bear to think about it. Every year that passed, Brandon seemed to recede into the distance, the quiet boy he remembered dancing away from him, the possibility of finding his son growing ever more faint.

He needed the oblivion of sensation, of Lori's touch. Rising, he pulled her to her feet and into his arms. He covered her mouth with his, wanting reality to disappear, for the nightmare of his missing son to vanish.

Taking Lori's hand, he led her up the stairs and into the house.

Chapter Thirteen

The bedroom door shut behind them, Gabe wanted everything at once—Lori naked, her legs wrapped around him, his hard flesh thrusting into her. His fingers tight around her upper arms, he held her still while he pushed his tongue into her mouth.

"Gabe…"

The feel of her breath on his cheek as she spoke only inflamed him more. He backed her toward the bed.

"Gabe!" This time she arched her body back, her hands pushing against his chest. "Slow down."

He stared at her, stunned. Forcing himself to take a breath, he stepped back from her.

"Need a minute." He headed for the bathroom, shut himself in the small room, threw handfuls of cold water on his face. The man he saw in the mirror looked like a stranger—crazed and angry, no doubt frightening as hell to Lori.

He ought to walk out of here, back to his own room. Hell, he'd climb in his truck and drive back home if Lori wasn't stranded here. She'd certainly be better off without him.

He heard the knob turn and the door opened

slowly. Lori stood there on the threshold, her face heartbreakingly beautiful, her eyes soft with concern.

"I was halfway to forcing you," he said, disgusted with himself.

"You weren't. Believe me, I know the difference."

There wasn't a shred of condemnation in her eyes. That only twisted the emotions in the pit of his stomach even tighter. "I should go."

"Come lie with me." She smiled, breaking down all his defenses. "We don't have to make love. Just come be with me."

How could he refuse? When she reached for him, opening herself to him? She was steady and clear-eyed at a moment he needed that stability desperately.

He followed her to the bedroom, and slipping off their shoes, they lay on the bed in each other's arms. Just having her close, feeling her warmth, her gentle curves under his hands, eased the rage. The darkness of the past still burned inside him, but with Lori he could hold that bleakness at bay.

Her head tucked against his shoulder, he felt her mouth move as she spoke. "My parents didn't understand anything but success. My older sister followed in their footsteps, always doing the right thing. I messed up over and over—acting out in school, cutting classes, hanging out with the wrong people. My parents fixed everything—with money whenever possible, with subtle threats of legal action if money didn't work."

Listening to Lori talk about her past was a relief, a way to stop revisiting his own. "Hightower's a pretty powerful force in Northern California."

"You could say that," she said wryly. "I didn't understand why I did what I did—I still don't. I think I sensed I would never succeed the way they wanted me to. It was less painful to run the other way, toward disaster."

"When I was a beat cop, I knew a lot of kids like you. Too much money, not enough responsibility."

She nodded agreement. "I was their beautiful little girl. They wanted to pretend I was as beautiful on the inside, that if they made everything easy for me, I would be able to do the right thing."

"Which was the worst thing they could have done."

"I know that now. And I know the responsibility to make it right is mine, not theirs."

A hawk screamed somewhere overhead, the cutting sound muted by the cocoon of the bedroom walls. "A hard lesson."

"I don't seem to do anything the easy way." She stroked his arm, sending warmth in the wake of her touch. "I discovered alcohol when I was fourteen. I'd drink to ease the pain, later to forget the pain had ever existed. Now my parents had something new to spend their money on—rehab."

"How many times?"

She sighed. "I lost count in my twenties. I never seemed to make it stick."

"Because it was their idea and not yours."

"Because they were pretty much doing it for me again." She pressed a kiss to his throat, sending sensation jetting down his spine. "I'd get stopped for DUI, they'd arrange to have it all go away with the promise of rehab. They'd drive me down there, pay extra to make sure I stayed on the straight and narrow, pick me up when it was over."

"And the moment you were out…"

"I'd take another drink."

Threading his fingers into her hair, he kissed her brow. "What finally changed?"

A shudder ran through her. "I nearly hit a car full of teenagers. Slammed into a light pole instead. Was lucky enough to escape with a few scratches."

"No parents to the rescue?"

"They would have been. They were in Europe at the time. They didn't find out until I'd stood up to the judge alone, made my own deal."

"Which was?"

"Go to A.A., stay sober on my own. If I slipped up even once, I'd put my own butt in jail."

He could see her standing in the courtroom, promising what every drunk promised—to stay sober. But she'd gutted it out and managed it for the past thirteen months.

"Your parents must be proud. To see you finally turn your life around."

He felt the tension in her. "I wouldn't know. I haven't seen them since."

His parents had been at times his only emotional support after Krista took Brandon. As agonizing as it had been to tell them their grandson was missing, as difficult as the years since had been, without their love he would have gone insane the past decade. He couldn't imagine handling the horror of it without them.

He drew his thumb along her jaw. "I know a little about the twelve steps. Number eight—"

"Become willing to make amends."

"And nine—"

"Make amends wherever possible." She shook her head. "It isn't possible right now. I'm afraid to be back in their world. Afraid I might go back to who I was."

He wanted to tell her she never would, that she'd keep on the path she'd set for herself. But how could he know? He'd lost his son, would likely never find him again. He had no crystal ball telling him where Brandon was hidden, how Lori's life would turn out.

He knew one thing with an absolute certainty—the feel of Lori's mouth against his, the silk of her hair, the satin of her skin. The single guarantee he had in life at that moment was Lori in his arms, ready to open herself to him.

Easing her back against the pillow, he kissed her, delicate touches that drew a sigh from her. But when he reached for the hem of her T-shirt to slip his hand under, she stopped him.

Her mouth curving into a smile, she pushed lightly against him, urging him onto his back. "My turn," she whispered.

Sitting up, she tugged his T-shirt from his jeans, her hands moving slowly, tantalizingly as she pushed it up along his chest. His flesh had already swelled with her in his arms, now he felt almost painfully tight, the feel of her fingers trailing across his skin beyond arousing.

He tried to grab her hands. "Lori—"

"My turn," she murmured again, taking his wrists, stretching his arms above his head. "You lie still."

Lying still was the last thing he wanted to do. She took her time pulling the T-shirt off, leaving it over his face while she dragged her tongue from one side to the other of his chest. She lingered on his flat nipples, teeth grazing, stealing his breath.

She uncovered his face again, tossing aside the T-shirt. Taking off her own shirt, she unhooked her bra, and when her breasts swung free he gave up breathing all together.

When he tried to reach for her, she pressed his hands back above his head. "Patience," she said.

Straddling his hips, she leaned down, letting her breasts brush his chest, until his heart thundered in his ears. He tightened his hands into fists as she lowered herself against him, the soft satiny mounds of her breasts setting him on fire.

His jaw tautened with the effort of keeping himself under control. "You're killing me here."

Her mouth close to his ear, she whispered, "I'm going to send you to heaven."

Her tongue traced his ear, his throat, along his jaw, to his mouth. She couldn't control his tongue, couldn't keep him from thrusting it into her mouth the way he wanted to thrust inside her body. She dueled with him, the heat of her mouth, her tongue tangling with his, setting the tension even tighter.

Finally, she shifted away from him and he felt her hand on the button of his jeans. Lowering the zipper far too slowly, her fingernails grazed his length through the knit of his shorts. He couldn't help himself; he thrust up toward her hand, wanting her so much he thought he'd go mad.

She eased his jeans from his hips slowly, drawing them down his legs, her fingers leaving a white-hot trail on his legs. By the time she returned to inch her fingertips under the waistband of his shorts, he thought he'd lose it before he got anywhere near where he wanted to be.

But she didn't touch his swollen flesh once she tugged down his shorts, just everywhere else around it, along his groin, his belly. He was rougher than he liked when he grabbed her wrist, but enough was enough.

"If you don't let me inside you right now," he growled, "this will be a very short party."

She smiled, but he saw the heat in her eyes. Edging from the bed, she shucked her jeans, peeling off the plain cotton panties. When he would have dragged her into his arms, she returned his hands above his head.

"It's still my turn," she whispered.

She found the second condom he'd left on the nightstand and lingered over the task of rolling it onto him. Straddling him again, she took his tight flesh in her hand and guided him inside her.

Buried in the moist warmth of her, he shut his eyes and took a breath, wanting to hold onto the incredible sensation as long as he could. Arched over him, she locked her hands with his and he opened his eyes to drink her in.

She was a goddess, a gift from heaven. It wasn't just the beauty of her face that moved him, it was the sweetness she possessed inside, the gentle dignity she carried with her. A man who had her by his side would truly be in heaven.

How could he let her leave?

The sudden realization of how it would feel to watch her walk away from him, to have her out of his life, cut like a sword in his side. She shouldn't mean anything to him, their chance meeting should have no significance to him. But somehow she'd become incredibly important in such a short time.

She started to move and everything but the feel of her evaporated from his mind. The wash of pink across her cheeks, the dusky color of her nipples against the cream of her breasts only intensified the rush of sensation. Her hold on his hands loosened, finally allowing him to touch her. He slid his palms up along her leg, wrapping his fingers around her hips to follow her motion as she rose and fell on him.

He didn't want to surrender to his climax, wanted instead to feel her tighten around him as she reached her peak. Bent over him, her arms shaking with the effort of supporting herself, she held back, drawing out the pleasure. Another moment of restraint and he'd be certifiable.

Hands tightening on her hips, he drove up into her, pushing himself as deep as he could. There was no holding back for either of them. Her climax triggered his, an incandescent explosion of heat searing his senses. The moment of passion seemed endless, too enormous to encompass. It filled him to overflowing, burst inside his heart.

Vulnerable, his soul stripped bare, he shut his eyes, needing a moment to restore the barriers he'd learned to build around himself. But he'd never contended with a force like Lori. When she relaxed against him, her body a balm against the pain of a decade, he didn't know if he had any defenses left.

He wanted to stay there forever, Lori in his arms, her sweet femininity always there to ease him from the hurricane of grief inside him. It was wrong; it wouldn't happen. But before he let her go, he could pretend there might be a happily ever after somewhere in his life.

Unwilling to let the moment stretch out too long, he edged away from her and went into the bathroom to clean up. He found himself hurrying back, still too ensnared by the paradise he'd experienced in that bed to resist climbing back in it.

When he lay beside her, she settled back in his arms. Her head against his shoulder, the silk of her hair stroked his neck, her fragrance tantalizing him. "You must be hungry," he said softly.

"I nibbled some crackers while you were in the bathroom." She spread her hand across his chest. "But I'll be starving pretty soon, probably demanding you make me lunch."

He drew his fingers along her side. "We spend much more time in here, it'll be closer to dinner."

She sighed. "I wish I never had to leave."

Don't leave. He squelched the longing inside him. He had to get up, get away from her before he got even more locked in by desires for things he could never have.

"I've got to go." He shifted away from her. "Have to get something done today."

He grabbed his clothes, keeping his back to her as he pulled them on. He didn't want to see whatever emotion was in her face. Yanking open the bedroom door, he heard the burbling of a cell phone.

He knew from the melody it was Lori's. He grabbed it from the breakfast bar, saw from the caller ID it was the body shop. When he turned to bring it to her, he stopped in his tracks. She'd followed him from the bedroom wearing only her T-shirt. With her mussed hair and bare feet, she was an irresistible turn-on.

She pressed the answer button on the phone and her head bent down as she spoke. He only dimly heard the conversation, too distracted by the long, long legs revealed below the hem of the T-shirt.

When she hung up, he had to drag his eyes up to her face. "Well?"

"My car is ready," she said. "I can pick it up any time."

Lori would have just as soon headed off to the body shop immediately to retrieve her car, but Gabe insisted she eat something first, telling her he damn well didn't want to deal with her passing out on him again. He seemed angry with her again, as if the intimacy of the morning meant nothing to him. He just seemed anxious to get her fed and back into town to get her car.

By the time they pulled out of the gravel drive, it was past three. She hadn't eaten much of the bowl of canned soup and French bread Gabe had thrown together for her, worried her emotional state coupled with the drive would bring on the nausea again.

Her emotions tumbled like clothes in a dryer, spinning and falling, changing too quickly to be identified. She didn't want to think about what she felt for Gabe, didn't want to consider how closely it seemed their lovemaking had linked them together. It was just her own confusion that led her to such crazy assumptions.

She didn't love him. She couldn't. It was just the aftermath of the lovemaking, the lingering sense of closeness that intimacy had brought.

Except she'd never felt this way before. All those

years drowning herself in alcohol and sex had meant less than nothing to her. With her ex-husband Tom, she'd felt protected, cared for, but not in love. And with Hugh the rat...she never really believed she loved him.

"You're not leaving today?" Gabe's voice pulled her from her reverie.

"There's no reason to stay." *Tell me you want me to stay.* The thought came unbidden.

"You might as well get a fresh start in the morning."

She looked over at him, saw nothing welcoming in the hard line of his jaw. A fervency burned in her to hear him say, *Stay with me, Lori. I need you in my life.*

"I'd rather just get on the road." She held her breath as she waited for his response.

He hit the brakes for a red light. "Suit yourself."

There was no reason to expect more from him. She would be fooling herself if she thought there was more between them than a brief interlude between two hungry bodies.

Still the ache settled deep inside her as they pulled into the body shop. She saw her little car parked off to one side, good as new. When Gabe stopped the truck, she couldn't get out of the cab quick enough.

He shut off the engine and she thought he might come inside with her. But he stayed put, barely visible through the truck's windshield once she was inside the shop. He waited until she came back outside and headed over to her Civic before starting the engine of the truck again.

His engine idling at the exit, he pulled back onto the highway once she was behind him. Driving her car for the first time since the accident, she felt edgy and anxious. She would have given anything to have Gabe in the seat beside her.

But nothing jumped out in front of her Honda, not so much as a squirrel. She pulled safely onto the access road to the chalet, still behind Gabe, a quiet grief overwhelming her at the prospect that she would be leaving him soon.

She wouldn't cry. That would just be disastrous.

She managed to get into the bedroom without looking at him, afraid that even a glance would trigger her tears. Pulling the door nearly shut, she had enough presence of mind to retrieve her suitcase from under the bed. Zipping it open, she stood there staring down at it, summoning the strength to open the dresser drawers and start packing.

She'd just put the last of her toiletries into the suitcase when she heard the trill of a cell phone from the kitchen. Reflexively, she started from the room before she realized it was Gabe's. Standing in the bedroom doorway, Gabe's back to her, she let herself look her fill while he spoke on the phone. She sensed his sudden tension more than saw it in the lines of his body.

The cell slipped from his hand and clattered to the floor. She didn't think, just closed the distance between them and put her hand on his arm. "What is it?"

He turned to her slowly, reaching for her hand. He hung onto her, his grip almost painfully tight. "That was Tyrell," he said hoarsely.

"What's wrong?" Sudden fear flared inside Lori. "Has something happened to Sadie?"

Gabe shook his head. "He thinks he's found my son."

Chapter Fourteen

Gabe couldn't seem to let her go. His world had just been slammed off its tracks and sent in an entirely different direction, and it was all he could do to keep his feet. If Lori hadn't been there, an anchor in the whirlwind spinning around him, he wasn't sure if he'd even be able to take his next breath.

"Where is he?" she asked him. When he didn't answer immediately, she gave his hand a shake. "Gabe."

"Near Phoenix." He could barely rasp out the word. "A mobile home park in Avondale."

"You have an address?"

Her question didn't register at first. When it did, he dove for the cell phone at his feet. "I didn't write it down."

Tyrell had given him the address, had spelled out the street name and the zip code slowly. But Gabe had been too numb to take it in, let alone grab paper and pen to write it down.

Stabbing out Ty's cell number, he fumbled the buttons and had to hit the clear key more than once. Meanwhile, Lori had torn a blank page from her journal and handed it to him along with a pen. She stood beside him, still his anchor, one hand on his arm.

"Hey, buddy," he said when Tyrell answered.

His friend didn't rib him over neglecting to write down the information. Tyrell understood the magnitude of what he was giving Gabe. Gabe wrote it carefully, then read it back to be sure.

"How'd you get this?" He hadn't had the presence of mind to ask before.

"A lucky break," Ty told him. "Remember Maria Ortiz? Joined the force not long before you left."

"Yeah, I think so." He had a dim recollection of a dainty, dark-haired woman.

"Maria moved to the Phoenix area a few years ago, joined the Avondale police department. She went out on a burglary call regarding a bike stolen from the front yard. Recognized Krista from the picture I keep at my desk."

"When?"

"Two days ago. Took her a while to remember where she'd seen Krista before."

"You're sure he was with her?" Gabe had already asked the question, but felt compelled to ask it again.

"He's the one who called it in. Maria questioned him about the bike. He looked enough like Brandon that she recognized him."

An ache settled in his chest. Would he know his son when he saw him? "I haven't finished the deck repairs."

"You think I care about that?" Ty said. "Get yourself to Phoenix."

Gabe said his goodbyes and folded the slip of paper, tucking it into his wallet. "Got to pack. Get a flight to Phoenix."

"You pack. I'll call the airline."

"Good. Thanks." He fished a credit card from his wallet and handed it to her before striding down the hall to his bedroom.

Opening dresser drawers, he grabbed handfuls of clothes and stuffed them into the duffel he'd brought. He dithered over whether to take his gun, then decided he'd have an easier time getting through airport security if he left it locked in the truck. His fishing gear was still out on the back deck but it would have to stay there until he could get back. Maybe he'd come up on weekends to finish the work on the deck.

Maybe Brandon would be with him.

His throat so tight he could barely breathe, he slung his holster over his shoulder and carried his duffel to the great room. Lori had her suitcase by the door with her purse and the stack of books she'd brought.

He almost stumbled when the magnitude of it hit him. He wouldn't see her again after today.

While he was trying to wrap his mind around that, she smiled at him, her expression unsure. "I made the reservations," she said. "For both of us."

Joy burst inside him, and he had to look away to keep her from seeing it in his face. Once he had himself under control, he turned back to her. "Okay. Let's go, then."

She returned his credit card. "I'll pay you back for my ticket."

"No, you won't." He turned away so she wouldn't argue the point, shoving his wallet into his back pocket and clipping his cell phone to his belt. Holster still over his shoulder, he grabbed his duffel and her suitcase. Books in one arm, she locked the door, and headed down the stairs.

When he started for his truck, she stopped him. "How about if I drive?"

"Yeah, good idea." He could barely keep his head straight, let alone muster enough concentration to drive. Securing his Glock in the glove box, he locked the truck and climbed into Lori's car.

As they pulled away from the chalet, he wished he could take her hand, desperately needing that connection. All the years he'd followed every lead, faced disappointment over and over, he'd never prepared himself for this—success. A very real possibility he would see his son again.

As she slowed for a traffic light, she gently touched his arm. "Tell me about him."

His throat closed and he didn't think he could say a word. To cover for the sudden surge of emotion, he drew his wallet from his back pocket and found the photo of Brandon he usually kept on his dash. He held it out to Lori.

"He looks like you," she said, and pride swelled inside him. "Especially the eyes."

Gabe gazed down at the photo in his hand. "He was always such a good little kid. He hardly cried as a baby. Too busy smiling."

His heart ached as he remembered those first moments in the morning when he'd reach for Brandon in his crib. The baby grin in response to his daddy's arrival never failed to put an answering smile on Gabe's face.

"I'd read to him after his bath. He'd be crawling around on his bedroom floor while I read *The Wizard of Oz* aloud to him. I doubt he paid attention to a word of it, but I just liked being with him."

Krista had never read to Brandon, had been grateful he took over their son's care when he got home from work. She'd be in the living room, zoning out in front of the television while he went through Brandon's nighttime rituals.

"That was the hardest to deal with after she took him. Thinking about him at bedtime, waiting for Daddy to read to him."

He shut his eyes, focusing on the rhythm of the wheels on the pavement, the sound of the car's engine. If he didn't blank his mind to the pain inside him, he wouldn't be able to hold back the tears. And damned if he would cry.

Lori's brief touch on his shoulder pulled him from the morass of grief that threatened. Opening his eyes, he reached across the car, lay his hand on her shoulder, giving in to his need for the contact. For now, he had to lean on her, had to draw on her strength. He still held Brandon's photo in his other hand, probably bending it irreparably. But soon, surely, he'd be seeing his son in the flesh.

The rest of the ninety-minute drive to the Reno Airport passed in silence. He kept his hand on her shoulder and once when she stopped at a traffic light, she lifted his hand to her mouth and pressed a kiss into his palm. Warmth spread inside him, a healing balm.

They arrived at the airport an hour and a half before departure, enough time to park Lori's car and make their way through check-in and security. Waiting to board was agonizing, the only relief Lori's hand locked in his.

As they stood in line at the gate, he kept her close to his side. "He won't know me. I have to accept that at the outset. I'll be a stranger to him."

"She might have told him about you."

Handing over the boarding passes, they headed down the Jetway. "If she told him anything, it would be lies. That I'm dead. Or some kind of monster."

Lori smiled up at him. "You'll win him over."

Gabe doubted it would be that easy, but he kept that opinion to himself. At least one of them ought to be optimistic.

She sat by the window and he took the middle seat, keeping her hand in his. With the first lurch of the plane as it backed from the gate, Gabe felt the tension tighten inside him.

"Even if he doesn't want me in his life," he said, grateful for Lori's touch, "I'll see him. I'll know he's okay."

"He'll love you, Gabe. How can he not?"

He raised his palm to her cheek and brushed her lips with his. As he rested his forehead against hers, emotion flooded him, feelings so overwhelming he wasn't about to explore them. It was gratitude, that was all, for Lori's support when his foundation had been knocked out from under him.

He drew back, looked into her soft brown eyes. He saw something there that jolted him, something that terrified him even more than the prospect of facing his son again. She didn't say a word, but he could see it nonetheless.

Settling back in his seat, he shut his eyes, neither wanting to accept nor reject what he'd seen in Lori's steady gaze. With any luck, she'd keep those feelings to herself. He wouldn't want to disappoint her, hurt her when he didn't feel the same way himself.

Or did he?

* * *

The one-hour layover in Los Angeles seemed endless, Gabe so restless it was all Lori could do to keep him seated on the plane once they boarded. She could feel the anxiety bursting from him when they finally took off from LAX, his hand so tightly locked in hers, she wondered if she'd ever be able to peel his fingers away.

He folded his other hand over hers. "We'll go straight from the airport to the house."

"If you want."

His fingers flexed as he turned his sharp gaze on her. "You don't think we should?"

She stroked his cheek with her free hand, wishing she could somehow ease his tension. "Whatever you decide is fine."

He stared down at their linked hands. "I was just thinking…by the time we get in, get the rental car, then drive the thirty minutes or so out to Avondale, it'll be ten, ten-thirty."

"I don't mind."

"But Brandon…" He tipped his head back up to her. "If we show up that late, two strangers on his doorstep…how will he feel? I don't want him scared."

She could see him working things through in his mind. He seemed a million miles away, lost somewhere in the clouds surrounding the aircraft.

His gaze fell on their hands locked together and for the first time since they'd left Reno, he let go. "I have to think about this. What's best for Brandon." As abruptly as that, he shut her out, as if suddenly aware of how much of himself he'd exposed to her.

She shouldn't be surprised, didn't even have the

right to feel the pain that dug deep inside her. *This doesn't mean commitment.* He'd been up front with her at the start. But even still she'd hoped, she'd longed for more.

Dropping her hands in her lap, she let her own gaze drift out the window, taking in long slow breaths to release the hurt inside her. The flight was just over an hour; she could spend that time focusing back on herself, the baby inside her, what she would do next.

The realization hit her so hard, she gasped, drawing Gabe's attention. "What's wrong?"

"Nothing, I…" A joy welled up inside her and she was suddenly filled with gratitude that she'd met Gabe, that he'd marked the path for her decision without even knowing it. *I'm keeping my baby. No matter what.*

She wanted to tell him, could barely hold the pronouncement inside. But knowing that the child inside her only painfully reminded him of his own son, she kept her epiphany to herself.

"Nothing," she repeated. His gaze roved her face a moment before he turned away again. Reclining his seat, he crossed his arms over his chest and with that gesture cut her off again.

She had to laugh inwardly at her own dismay. Almost like a child, she'd wanted Gabe to press her, then to assure her she'd made the right choice. That Gabe's acknowledgment of her decision meant more to her than anyone else's—even Amy's—just made clearer the folly of thinking she meant something to him.

She knew nothing about love. She couldn't if she thought the swelling emotion inside her was her love for Gabe. She simply cared for him as a fellow human being, wanted him to find happiness, joy in his life. If that meant helping him locate his son, she would do it, because it was what one caring person would do for another.

She looked over at him, hungrily traced the lines of his profile, the set of his shoulders. She wanted more than anything to take his hand again, connect with him, somehow reach inside him. She wanted him with her instead of just beside her. But he'd built his walls up again and she didn't know how to reach him.

Maybe she shouldn't have come with him at all. She'd thought she could be a support, could offer strength. But in that moment, she felt she needed his strength. She needed his confirmation that keeping her baby was right. Even though she knew she had to make that decision on her own.

She wished that just once in her past, she'd truly loved, so she could understand what she felt for Gabe. She loved her daughter so much it almost hurt inside. She would do anything for Jessie—even stay out of her life if that was best for her.

But her intimacy with Gabe had tangled everything up. Their physical closeness had been a piece of heaven she'd never experienced before. It had meant so much more than any other encounter with a man, it wasn't even in the same universe. But when did those sublime sensations translate into love?

And if she did love him, then what? Pour her heart out to him just to have him remind her she'd promised no strings? Or keep it to herself, and let him go after he'd found his son? That possibility stabbed at her so painfully, she couldn't bear thinking about it.

By the time the plane landed at Phoenix Sky Harbor airport, she'd given herself permission to simply let the problem be. Whether she loved him or not didn't matter, because either way, she'd have to say goodbye to him soon. What she felt for Gabe fell into the category of something she couldn't change. She hoped she had the courage to accept that.

When they climbed into the small sedan Gabe had rented, he didn't start the engine right away. Hands on the wheel, he stared out the windshield.

"I don't think we should go tonight," he said quietly. "I think it would be better in the light of day."

"Okay."

Not sure of her welcome, she put her hand on his shoulder. He tensed at first, then let out a sigh. "Being so close to him, it's almost too much to take in."

She gave his shoulder a squeeze. "We should probably get a room."

"Yeah. Guy at the rental counter gave me a list."

He started the engine and pulled out of the lot. The lights of Phoenix spread in every direction, the occasional saguaro reaching its arms up to heaven.

There was something lonely about the tall cacti dotting the landscape. Or maybe it was just her own isolation she felt so sorely. She imagined herself and Gabe as saguaros out in the desert, each of them alone and self-contained, arms reaching up, searching heaven for answers. If they could only reach across the space between them, maybe they could help each other.

She looked over at him, saw the barriers between them and felt more lost than ever.

* * *

If he had an ounce of brains, he would have reserved two rooms. As he unlocked the door and pushed inside, Lori just behind him, he couldn't figure out where his good sense had gone. One room, a king-size bed—it was lunacy.

Still he had to do the noble thing. "We don't have to do anything…" He set aside her suitcase. "I don't want you to feel you have to."

She just stared at him as if he was insane. They both knew what would happen in that bed. It wasn't as if the passion they'd felt at the chalet had relented. The anticipation of seeing his son tomorrow, the myriad emotions tied to that event, only heightened his desire for her. The temporary oblivion of sensation provided too great a lure.

That was all he wanted from her, physical sensation. Not a hand to hold in the dark moments, a strong, caring woman at his side to revel in the good times, struggle together through the bad. That was the province of love. He'd abandoned that territory the day Krista took his son.

He'd realized on the plane he'd let himself get too close to Lori, too dependent on her to soothe his suffering. He'd let himself forget that their time together wouldn't endure past the next day or so. If he kept hanging on, continued to draw on her for support, it would only make matters worse when they parted.

Pulling away had been painful, but necessary. It wasn't right to lead her to believe there was something between them when their alliance was only temporary. She hadn't touched him since that moment in the car when she saw his need for comfort.

Yet he'd only asked for one room. He felt like such a bastard for continuing to let her give to him when he had no intention of giving back. But the situation pulled him in a hundred directions at once until he thought he'd explode from the tension. If Lori hadn't been here to calm him, he might have barreled over to Krista's and done God knows what to his ex-wife.

Her toiletries bag in her hand, Lori ducked into the bathroom and shut the door. He heard the lock turn. No doubt with his hot and cold treatment of her, she felt she needed the privacy.

Cranking on the AC, he flipped on the television and switched through the stations with the remote. He stopped at a ballgame and saw it was the Diamondbacks playing extra innings in L.A. He and Brandon could be watching the game, sharing a bowl of popcorn and cans of root beer.

He heard the shower start up, sidetracking him from the high pop fly on the screen. He pretty much knew every inch of that body in the shower, had explored it from head to toe. But if there was any way to get enough of Lori Jarret, he didn't know it. If the door hadn't been locked, he'd be in there with her, pressing her wet, soapy body to his.

Shoving off his shoes, he sat back on the bed, propping the pillows behind him. He doubted that bathroom lock would take more than a few moments to jigger open from the outside. He knew half a dozen ways to take care of it. He wouldn't—she'd made it clear she wanted the time alone—but the temptation teased him nonetheless.

The Diamondbacks grounded to second for the third out and the Dodgers took the field. He muted the television—it wasn't as if he was paying much attention to the game, anyway. So when the shower shut off he could hear it, when she pushed aside the plastic curtain, he caught the scrape of the rings on the rod. The image of her stepping from the tub, wet and pink from the hot water, floated in his mind's eye.

One pitch later, the Dodgers popped one over the fence and the tie game was over. Snapping off the television, he listened for her, his heart hammering when he heard the click of the lock. When she stepped out, a faint cloud of scented steam drifted over to him.

Wrapped in a towel, she snatched up her suitcase and vanished back in the bathroom before he got much more than a glimpse. By the time she returned, she wore a ridiculous flannel nightgown.

"You'll roast in that."

"I'm fine."

He considered arguing the point, but maybe it was just as well. The less he could see of her body, the better.

He got up and headed for the bathroom himself. On the way, he snagged a pair of sweat shorts from his suitcase. He tried not to think about her in the shower with him, but as he stripped off his T-shirt and jeans, his body was hard and ready for her.

He made short work of his shower, blasting himself with cold water at the end. When he went back into the room, the sweat shorts doing a lousy job of hiding his heat for her, she was in bed, already under the covers, facing the wall.

At least she'd discarded the flannel nightie. Turning off the lights, he dropped the shorts and climbed under the sheet. When he reached for her, the sheet stopped him, blocking him from her.

"You're on top of the sheet."

"I'm taking you at your word. That we don't have to." She turned toward him. "Unless you didn't mean it."

He hadn't, at least hadn't expected that she'd go along with his gallantry. "The sheet isn't necessary. I won't touch you at all if you don't want me to."

"I just need some time to take things in. Settle things in my mind."

"I want you." He pushed his hardness against her hip. "I think I've pretty much settled that."

"I know. It's just…" Her breath feathered across his cheek. "Tonight just hold me. Be near me."

It was like a fist to his chest. The intimacy of having her in his arms without the sex, without arousing her and bringing her to climax was more intense that simply the physical release. The prospect shook him, made him want to scramble from the bed, run from the room.

Yet how could he leave her? She was everything he wanted, at least at that moment, at least for that night. There was no way he could turn away what she offered.

"Then I'll hold you," he whispered in the dark. Shifting on the other side of the sheet, she lay against him, her hips lightly against his. With his flesh heated and ready for her, it was difficult to think, so he didn't, he just let the emotions go.

He could love her tonight. A temporary love, a transitory love. He could give himself these few hours. Then later he'd let her go.

Chapter Fifteen

Lori made it clear she was driving the next morning, taking the car keys from the dresser without comment. As she stepped out into the bright Phoenix sunshine, the temperature already in the low eighties, Gabe followed behind with the suitcases, setting them in the trunk she opened for him. He headed for the passenger side without argument.

He was wound so tight he hadn't eaten much more than a bite or two of the continental breakfast the hotel provided in the lobby, just gulped coffee and stared out the window. Once in the car, he pulled out the address Tyrell had given him, then scanned the directions to Avondale he'd gotten from the desk clerk.

"I called the school," he told her as they navigated the surface streets toward Interstate 10. "They're already out for the summer."

"So he should be home."

"Yeah." He smoothed the directions across his denim-clad leg. "Should be."

She pulled onto the freeway and immediately slowed for rush hour traffic. "Do you think she'll be there?"

He released a long gust of air. "Maybe. If she hasn't gone to work. If she even has a job."

Her resolve to merely sleep with Gabe last night without making love had been tested sorely when she woke to his hands on her, his mouth hot on her throat. She'd turned to him, impatient with the sheet between them and would have pushed it away with one more kiss, one more touch.

But then the tantalizing motion of his fingers slowed and he pressed a last kiss beneath her ear. His breathing evened and she would have thought he'd fallen asleep if she hadn't seen the faint gleam of his open eyes.

His fingers grazed her shoulders. "Take the Ninety-ninth Avenue exit and turn left."

They reached Ninety-ninth Avenue a few minutes later and pulled off the freeway. "Right on Buckeye," Gabe read from the sheet. "It turns into Main Street."

Lori slowed as she saw the mobile home park up ahead. Beside her, Gabe had rumpled the sheet of paper in his hand.

They turned into the driveway, easing along the roadway at a crawl. Lori stopped at a kiosk for a map of the park. "What was the unit number?"

"Two-oh-four." He said the words in a bare whisper.

Following the map, Lori continued on, finally stopping at unit 204. Hands fisted in his lap, Gabe stared at the single-wide mobile between two other nearly identical homes.

"I can stay here," Lori said quietly.

"Yeah," he answered just as softly.

He opened his door, made to step out, then reached for her hand. Eyes closed, he pressed a kiss to the back of her hand, then lifted his gaze to hers again.

"I want you to know…" His green eyes skimmed her face. "When you told me about your daughter, about your past…the fact that you didn't keep it hidden, that you admitted all of it, even the worst of it…" His fingers tightened. "That took incredible courage. That you want to change it, make it right… I've never known a braver woman than you."

With that he released her hand and slipped from the car, leaving Lori in stunned silence, trying to grasp what he'd just said. Even as her heart sang at his vote of confidence, she couldn't begin to understand the motivation behind it.

She watched through the windshield as he climbed the wooden steps of the porch. Crossing to the door, he stood for several seconds before he finally opened the screen and knocked. When there was no answer, he knocked again.

He peered inside the window beside the door, then finally turned back toward the car. Lori stepped out as he descended the stairs.

"No one's home." He looked around the park, as if hoping to find Brandon somewhere nearby.

Lori drew her hand down his arm, the muscles rigid with tension. "Maybe they've just gone out."

She caught a glimpse of a curtain pushed aside in the unit next to two-oh-four, then heard the clatter of a front door opening. An old woman poked her head out and shouted, "You looking for that woman and her boy?"

Gabe pulled away from Lori, moving to the bottom of the old woman's porch steps. "Do you know them?"

"Kept to themselves, mostly. Didn't say so much as howdy to me more than once or twice."

"Do you know when they'll be back?" Gabe asked.

Lori knew what was coming, had rounded the car and set a path straight to Gabe. She hadn't quite reached him when the old woman answered.

"Won't be back. They cleared out of here for good two days ago. Piled everything they owned in their car and skedaddled."

If he hadn't been holding the stair rail, his knees would have given way. As it was, he sank to the bottom step, not an ounce of strength left. Lori appeared beside him, her fingers locking with his, an anchor in the maelstrom of emotion assaulting him.

"Two days ago," he said numbly.

"Could she have recognized the policewoman?"

He shook his head. "Maria wasn't with LAPD back then." But as paranoid as Krista was, she would have imagined danger from anyone in uniform.

"They can't have gone far. You can still find them."

"You think they left a forwarding address?" He laughed, the sound harsh to his own ears. "Not likely."

"There has to be a way." She got to her feet and returned to the car. Retrieving the pink sheet of paper with the mobile park layout on it, she studied it a moment before grabbing her cell phone.

The old woman had gone back inside, but he could feel her stare from the front window. Pushing himself up, he reclimbed the stairs, wanting to linger where his son had so recently lived.

Finishing her call, Lori joined him on the porch. "The park manager is on his way. He'll let us in."

He knew he likely wouldn't find anything inside, at least nothing that would clue him in as to where Krista was going next. She'd covered her tracks so well these past ten years, why would she be any less thorough this time?

He barely held despair at bay as the mobile park manager arrived with the key and unlocked the door. "Haven't had a chance to clean this unit," the older man said, "but you young folks can take a quick peek."

As they stepped inside the compact space, Gabe scanned the small living room with its ratty sofa and easy chair, scratched coffee table and end tables. Even with the glaring sun penetrating the gauzy curtains on the windows, the room seemed dank and depressing. He couldn't stand that his son had lived in this place.

The manager had stayed out on the porch, so Gabe and Lori went through the unit on their own. Gabe checked in kitchen drawers, under the sofa cushions, in the closets of the tiny bedrooms. Crammed into one of the nightstands of the back bedroom—Krista's room?—he found a rumpled sheet of paper with a crudely rendered child's drawing in crayon.

It was signed "Brandon," and featured a stick figure family of a mommy and her little boy. A hole had been torn out of the picture, leaving only part of the head of a third figure. Daddy?

His eyes felt wet as he stared down at the drawing. Lori, who'd been going through the bathroom, came up behind him. "What did you find?"

"Nothing." He folded the sheet and carefully tucked it into a back pocket. "Let's get out of here."

As he'd suspected, there was nothing left to find, nothing to point him anywhere. Brandon was just as lost to him now as he'd always been. It only hurt that much more because they'd come so close.

He dragged in a breath as they climbed back in the car. "When does our flight leave today?"

"Not until four." Lori started the car. "Where to next?"

"The school. Not likely she left a forwarding address there, but…" He had to at least go through the motions.

The clerk at the middle school was sorry to hear Brandon had moved. He was always well-behaved, she said, worked hard. No, she didn't even know they'd gone, let alone where they might be going.

Back at the car, Gabe felt as if his world was closing in on him, inch by inexorable inch. He felt like a wounded animal desperate for cover, for comfort. The last thing he wanted to do was go to Lori again for that consolation.

"What now?" she asked, even her soft voice a temptation to give in to her.

"The airport," he said roughly. "I want out of here, now."

They managed to get an earlier flight, the fifty dollar change fee for each ticket a small price to pay to leave Phoenix behind. By the time they made it through security, the attendant was making a last call for boarding and they ran the last twenty yards to the gate. Ten minutes later, the plane was pulling away.

"I'll be staying in L.A.," he told her as the plane took off. "I want to check in with Tyrell, see if he has any ideas."

"I can stay with you." Her gentle voice set off a longing inside him.

"No, thanks. I won't be needing your help anymore."

He winced inwardly at how cold he sounded, how harsh. But he didn't see the point in softening the blow. They'd always intended to go their separate ways. Why draw it out now?

Still, he could sense the hurt radiating from her and couldn't help but feel guilt digging at him. He longed to look into her eyes again, to see that beautiful light shining. But that would be a huge mistake. It was better to cut himself off from her, right here, right now.

"I need some shut-eye," he told her. "I didn't sleep well last night."

He turned away from her as best he could in the narrow seat and closed his eyes. Her fragrance drifted toward him, setting off an ache inside him. He had to accept that although he could shut her out of his life, he would never completely banish her from his heart.

Lori heard the first boarding call for her flight from Los Angeles to Reno and rose from her seat to head for the gate. Gabe, who'd posted himself several feet away as if he couldn't bear to be near her, fell in beside her.

"You can go now," Lori said, barely louder than a whisper.

"In a minute." He moved along with her as the line snaked to the gate. "Look, I'm sorry."

"For what?"

"For…" He made an impatient gesture. "It was a mistake. All of it. I never should have—"

"*We* never should have." They were nearly to the gate. "No regrets, Gabe. You can go back to your life with a free conscience."

Then she was handing over the boarding pass and striding down the Jetway. Quickly finding her seat, she stowed her purse and buckled herself in, trying to force her mind into blankness. Before she could stop herself, a fleeting fantasy popped into her mind— Gabe running onto the plane, stopping her before it left the gate.

But the slamming of the door and the lurch of the jet as it edged backward destroyed the childish bit of whimsy. She gripped the armrests, tensed her body to keep the tears away as the jet taxied, waiting to take off. She refused to let them fall, despite the ache in her throat, the weight settled on her heart.

She'd known from the start there'd be no future for them. He'd promised nothing, she'd sworn to him she expected nothing. He might have been kinder to her than most of the men she'd tangled with, more honest. He'd certainly respected her more. But that didn't change the final result. Theirs was a brief interlude, a temporary paradise. Now it was over.

How could she fall in love with him?

The plane's acceleration as it took off pushed her back into the seat, adding to the heaviness in her chest. She wished she could fly away, farther than the jet could possibly take her, to the stars, the farthest galaxy. Anything to escape the pain, the unrelenting grief.

She was selfish to the last. Gabe had real grief to contend with—the loss of his son. What worse nightmare could a parent have? In the past year since she'd started the dance back into her daughter's life, she'd realized how important Jessie was to her, how powerful her love was for the strong-willed little girl. She couldn't imagine how it would feel to have Jessie vanish, truly out of reach. At least Lori still had the hope of rebuilding a bridge between herself and her daughter. Gabe might never have that chance with his son.

The hour-and-ten-minute flight to Reno seemed endless, the persistent tears at the corners of her eyes tightening her throat. Once she disembarked, she felt a little better, able to let go of the grip of loneliness a bit as she claimed her baggage and walked to her car.

But once she climbed into her Civic and took a breath to hold back the tears, she caught a hint of Gabe's scent lingering in the car. There was no restraining the emotion then, her sobs taking hold of her like an animal digging its claws in deep. Hanging on to the steering wheel as if it were a lifeline, she wept in the parking lot until she had no tears left.

She felt weak and shaky when she started the car and realized she hadn't eaten since breakfast. Gabe had tried to force some food on her at LAX as they'd waited for her flight, but she'd only managed a bite or two. She had to stop for gas anyway; she might as well grab something to eat, too.

Once she'd refueled herself and her car, she headed back to the city via Interstate 80. The temptation to divert her route through South Lake Tahoe instead was powerful. She thought maybe if she could see the chalet one more time, it might bring some closure to her heart. But she had to admit to herself it would only make matters worse to see the place without Gabe there.

As she zigzagged along the curves of Interstate 80, still fighting tears, she realized that struggling against what she felt for Gabe was harder than simply accepting it. She'd fallen in love with him, without meaning to, against the odds. Because he was at his core a good man, because she was finally seeing clearly without the haze of alcohol veiling her from the world. Despite the pain of not having that love returned, she was grateful for feeling it nonetheless. It was an important step on her path to finally growing up and taking charge of her own life.

By loving Gabe, she'd proved she *could* love, that she could step outside herself and feel for someone else. Although she couldn't imagine it in that moment, someone else could come along, a man as willing to give to her as she was to him. Now she knew she was ready to build a life with someone else.

Acknowledging her love did loosen the ache around her heart, made the loneliness easier to bear. She would be a long time getting over him, but had plenty to distract her—preparing for the baby, rebuilding the bridges with Jessie, working at the teen center. She had a full, incredible life to look forward to. She just had to accept that Gabe would never be part of it.

Arranging his month's leave from the Marbleville County sheriff's department had been tricky. Summer always meant more work for the deputies, what with kids out of school and vacationing tourists getting themselves lost in the woods around Hart Valley. But once Gabe told Sheriff Larkin about Brandon, for the first time revealing what he'd kept hidden for the six years he'd been sheriff's deputy, he got the time off on the spot.

He just needed to find a way to get himself back together after the crushing disappointment of the trip to Phoenix. He'd intended to hole up in a hotel alone, but Ty and Sadie King would have none of that. They put him up at their place, magically rearranged their schedules so that nearly always one of them was home with him. They pretty much coddled him as if he were a sickly two-year-old. He put up with it for a week, then finally insisted they get back to their lives.

The grief over losing Brandon again after coming so close eased somewhat during his time in L.A., although he knew he would never let go of his son, even if he never saw him again. It was comforting to know his boy was still alive, that he did well in school, that others thought well of him. At the same time, Gabe had come to understand that he had to step back into life, that if he continued to wrap his entire being around finding Brandon, he would never be truly alive.

But as the days passed, stretching into two weeks, then three, Gabe discovered that while he could let go of the dream of finding his son, there was someone he could never let go. She was still lodged in his heart, a constant presence, a balm to his soul. Locating his son might be an impossibility. Lori wasn't.

With four days left of his month's leave, he found himself back in northern California. Between the flight to Reno and the trip to the chalet via car service to retrieve his truck, it was after 6:00 p.m. by the time he headed out to San Francisco. It would be nearly ten before he reached the city.

Sadie had been reluctant at first to give Gabe Lori's address. She'd apparently been in touch with Lori and knew a little of what had transpired between them at the chalet.

"I don't want her hurt," Sadie had said.

"That's the last thing I want," Gabe had assured her. "I just want to talk. If she wants me gone, if she doesn't feel for me the way I thought she did...I'll leave."

Now, as he parked his truck in a public lot near Lori's Noe Valley apartment, he realized he might have lied to Sadie. Because if Lori told him she didn't feel the way he did, he wasn't sure he could walk away.

Climbing the stairs to her second-floor apartment, his stomach clenched tight at the prospect of seeing her again. As late as it was, she might already be in bed and he felt a twinge of guilt that he might wake her. But he couldn't bear the thought of waiting until tomorrow to see her.

He located her apartment, rapped on the heavy door. He heard her call, "Just a minute," then her footsteps coming nearer. There was a hesitation and he assumed she was checking through the peephole to see who had knocked, then several moments passed while she no doubt considered whether she wanted to see him at all.

He thought his heart would stop when she finally opened the door. Then it shifted into overdrive with his first glimpse of her.

"Hi, sweetheart." The endearment came out without conscious will.

"Hello, Gabe."

"Can I come in?"

She slowly stepped aside and let him pass through.

When she shut the door, she leaned against it, one hand covering her belly.

"You're starting to show." He had to resist the urge to place his hand beside hers, to see if he could detect movement.

"What do you want, Gabe?"

There was no condemnation in her voice, but no encouragement either. He was on his own.

He shoved his hands into his jeans pockets to keep from touching her. "This might mean nothing to you. You might not even care." He took in a breath. "But I have to tell you anyway, have to at least take the chance."

He saw a brightness in her eyes, the beginnings of tears. He didn't know what the hell that meant, but he couldn't stop now.

"I love you, Lori. So much I want to shout it, tell everyone I see. I thought if I ignored it, it would go away, but it didn't. It won't."

"Oh, Gabe…" The tears spilled down her face and for a single horrifying instant, he thought she was about to turn him away. Then she uttered a miracle. "I love you, too."

He pulled her into his arms, kissing her face, running his hands over her body. He was afraid to let her go, terrified she might vanish like his son did a decade ago. But she was real, and she wasn't going anywhere.

"I would have let you go," she whispered. "But I couldn't stop loving you."

"You've kept me sane these past few weeks. Even four hundred miles away, I could love you and that kept me strong."

She leaned back, gazed up at him. "I'm so sorry about Brandon."

Brushing aside her tears, he kissed her brow. "Thank you. But I've got to go on."

"I'm beside you, Gabe. Every step of the way."

He cradled her face with his hands. "Marry me, Lori. I can move here if you want—"

"It's time I moved back to Hart Valley. I have unfinished business there."

"The baby—"

"I'm keeping him. Or her," she said, flashing her amazing smile. "You helped me figure that out."

He pulled her close, his arms enfolding her and the baby she carried. In that moment, the emptiness he'd carried inside for ten years started to fill up again. Brandon could never be replaced, but someone new could take his or her place beside his son's memory.

Emotion overwhelmed him, a gratitude that he'd found her. "I love you, Lori."

"I love you, too."

"Forever," he told her fervently.

Now his life could begin again.

Epilogue

Lori Walker sat on a redwood bench on the wide back porch of her and Gabe's Hart Valley cabin, sheltered by a sturdy overhang as a misty spring drizzle wet the grassy yard. At the other end of the porch, Jessie sprawled in a lounge chair, absorbed in a thick fantasy novel by her favorite author. Lori had given it to Jessie for Christmas and her daughter had pretty much worn it out rereading the paperback.

It had been nearly a year since her time with Gabe at the chalet. It had taken until the fall for her and Jessie to come to an understanding. There was nothing Lori could do to change the past, and all the apologies in the world would never lessen the severity of her transgressions. They'd agreed they would focus on the present, start over as best they could, forgiving and letting go.

Jessie still wasn't effusive in her affection for her mother. Lori had to accept that her daughter might always feel closer to her stepmother Andrea than she did to Lori. But Jessie was willing to let Lori into her life and for a twelve-year-old soon-to-be teenager, that was all Lori could hope for. In any case, she was enjoying getting to know her daughter.

It helped that Jessie adored her new stepfather. They'd bonded so quickly, Lori had been torn between jealousy for the ease with which they'd accepted one another and joy over their excellent relationship. Jessie was thrilled as well when the baby came, eager to help take care of her brand-new sister.

Lori heard faint cries from inside the house and Jessie jumped to her feet. "I'll get her."

"Gabe's got it handled, sweetie. He'll bring her out."

After Giselle was born, Gabe adopted her, wanting to make the baby whose birth he'd so eagerly anticipated officially his. Hugh had been happy to rid himself of the responsibility and didn't put up any objections. Amy had expedited the matter, and had gotten the adoption finalized in record time.

Lori's parents had welcomed their latest grandchild with a surprising warmth, their acceptance of their new son-in-law gratifying. When they were ready to set up generous trust funds for both Giselle and Jessie, Lori put her foot down, insisting the children needed the chance to earn their own way. Her parents reluctantly agreed.

Lori smiled as Gabe brought their three-month-old daughter out on the porch and immediately relinquished her to her impatient older sister. Just as well, since it allowed Gabe to come share the bench with her.

He snuggled up beside her, his warm body next to her still an exciting enticement. He brushed his mouth against her ear. "What do you say we let Jessie and her friend Sabrina babysit and you and I go to Marbleville for dinner?"

Sensation simmered up her spine. "I like your thinking."

She leaned her head on his shoulder, loath to move when she heard the phone ringing. She turned to her older daughter. "Jess, can you get that?"

Carrying her sister, Jessie headed into the house. Taking advantage of the moment of privacy, Gabe gave her a hot kiss, his tongue diving deep. They were so involved in the moment, they didn't hear Jessie return until she yelled Gabe's name.

Giselle tucked on her shoulder, Jessie waved the portable phone at him. "It's for you. Some kid."

Gabe turned to her, puzzled. Lori's heart beat faster when she realized who the caller could be.

When Gabe told her he'd entered his and Brandon's names on dozens of missing children Web sites over the years, she'd started searching for new places on the Internet to try. She'd stumbled across a new site just a month ago, one he hadn't yet registered with. The Web page used a cutting-edge search engine to consolidate and cross-reference parent and child names across the Web, but it had still been such a long shot she hadn't mentioned it to him.

"Who is it?" Gabe asked Jessie.

Jessie lifted the phone to her ear and asked the question, then held it out to Gabe. "He says his name is Brandon."

At first Gabe sat frozen, immobile. Then he turned to her, hope budding in his face. She smiled at him and nodded.

Hurrying across the porch, he grabbed the phone from Jessie. His gaze locking with Lori's, his voice strong, he said hello to his son.

* * * * *